GU00480693

A Little Bit of Heaven

For Briege Lavery of Woodside Queens N.Y. and
Ethna McKiernan of Minneapolis Minnesota
for exemplary help and guidance

Published in 1999 by
Mercier Press
5 French Church Street Cork
Tel: (021) 275040; Fax (021) 274969
E-mail: books@mercier.ie
16 Hume Street Dublin 2
Tel: (01) 661 5299; Fax: (01) 661 8583
E-mail: books@marino.ie

Trade enquiries to CMD Distribution
55A Spruce Avenue
Stillorgan Industrial Park
Blackrock County Dublin
Tel: (01) 294 2556; Fax: (01) 294 2564
E-mail: cmd@columba.ie

Cover design by
Penhouse Design Group
Printed in Ireland by ColourBooks,
Baldoyle Industrial Estate, Dublin 13

This book is sold subject to the
condition that it shall not, by way of
trade or otherwise, be lent, resold,
hired out or otherwise circulated
without the publisher's prior consent
in any form of binding or cover other
than that in which it is published and
without a similar condition including
this condition being imposed on the
subsequent purchaser.

© Introduction Sean McMahon 1999
The acknowlegements page is an
extension of this copyright notice.

No part of this publication may be
reproduced or transmitted in any
form or by any means, electronic or
mechanical, including photocopying,
recording or any information or
retrieval system, without the prior
permission of the publisher in writing.

ISBN 1 85635 250 1

10 9 8 7 6 5 4 3 2 1

A CIP record for this title is available
from the British Library

A Little Bit of Heaven

An Irish-American Anthology

Edited by
Sean McMahon

ᗰ ERCIER PRESS

Ireland and America

Dan Nash

(Mid-19th Century)

I love my native country,
I cannot be to blame,
And every man, no matter who,
I think should do the same.
The Yankee loves Columbia
Like true friends we'll combine,
For Yankeemen and Irishmen
Their hearts and hands should join.

When the Stars and Stripes
Shield the Shamrock sublime,
And America and Ireland in friendship combine,
Then we will show
When our flags are unfurl'd
That America and Ireland
Can face all the world.

Our interests are both the same,
That you can plainly see;
And there should be no reason
Why we should disagree.
Place both upon a footing,
And the world we can defy,
And if foes think to conquer us
They'd better come and try.

Contents

4 Wakes and Weddings
and Every County Ball

5 The Fighting Race

6 My Irish Molly, O

7 On Stage, Everybody!

8 A Great Day for the Irish

Introduction

In 1537, less than half a century after Columbus first descried Watling's Island in the Bahamas, a ship left Waterford for Newfoundland, the 'land of the fish'. It was the beginnings of a pattern of emigration from Ireland to the New World that was to continue until the present day. The eighteenth century saw a steady stream of mainly Ulster Presbyterians whose sense of adventure and grievance had them embrace the idea of seeking religious freedom, an end to political disability and worldly wealth in the 'colonies', and they played a significant part in the War of Independence which created the United States of America. The step westward was for many simply an extension of the earlier move that their forebears had made across the narrow sea from Scotland to plant where the native Irish had been displanted. Their expectation of conflict with savage aboriginals was about the same as that of the planters with the Irish. They brought with them as part of their cultural baggage the Bible and Kethe's *Metrical Psalms* and perhaps some folk memory of pre-Reformation dance music. Certainly in 'remote' places of settlement like the long knuckles of the Appalachians (which included the Blue Ridge mountains of Virginia) they combined with other settlers to lay the foundations of 'country' music. They played the fiddle and danced modified sets re-membered from what was not quite 'the old country', but since they travelled mainly as families they were God-fearing and, more important socially, respectable.

Presbyterians were not the only Protestant young people to go west; Anglicans, too, braved the misery of the ships and the dangers of the passage. Though not subject to political disability at home they responded as did many other Europeans to the instinct to seek a newer world where 'things might be better.' The emigrating Irish had the advantage of speaking the language of the new land which was a scarcely different English from the one they spoke but with a tendency to be conservative about vocabulary.

And then there were the Catholics . . . Political disability and penal enactments had tended to ennervate them but still some managed to save money or gain passage as indentured servants. They embraced the new country like the rest, in a sense disappearing into its fastness. America was, by the end of the first international war (between Napoleonic France and various European powers) in 1812, in spite of the terms of its high-minded Jeffersonian declaration, essentially white, Anglo-Saxon and Protestant.

With the slump at the end of the Napoleonic Wars the emigrants from Ireland no longer came largely from Protestant Ulster. By the time the potato blight (originating ironically in America) was about to cause an apocalyptic disaster to the staple food of millions of Irish at home there were nearly half a million Irish in the New World. They were not the poorest; and the demeanour of the Catholics was unthreatening. Among them were the lawyers, journalists, doctors and priests who put in place Irish-Catholic communities in Boston, New York, Philadelphia and Chicago that were eventually able to withstand the huge Famine influx of the 'unrespectable' – the very poor. These for a score of years, at least, because of their numbers, their wretchedness, their tendency to create shanty-town ghettos noted for violence and drunkenness, their willingness to work for less and to strike-break, were seen as a social scourge. Political cartoonists like Thomas Nast delighted to portray the Famine immigrants as simian subhumans. Pictures of Paddy climbing ladders with overloaded hods were captioned as 'I'm rising in the world', those of slatternly, near cretinous chambermaids read, 'I'm staying in the Grand Hotel,' and drawings of miserable shanties were labelled, with ironic accuracy, 'We're living in Fifth Avenue.'

The 'respectable' Irish were not yet known as 'lace-curtain' but their entertainments were as decorous as those of the Protestant middle class on both sides of the Atlantic. In the 1860s and 1870s their parlours had the same pianos and sheet music as their WASP neighbours, with Moore's *Melodies* leading the rest. Later, such pieces as J. L. Molloy's 'Bantry Bay', 'The Kerry Dances' and 'Love's Old Sweet Song' were sung with tears both by those who actually remembered the 'old country' and those for whom it was beginning to be a mythology. It was for these that 'Come back to Erin', 'Killarney' and 'I'll Take You Home Again, Kathleen' became almost hymns. These Irish-Americans kept an eye on the distressful country and involved themselves intermittently with political events there. When 'green' politics began to be significant it was always possible to find support Stateside for such home movements as the Irish Republican Brotherhood, the Land War, the 1916 Rising and the Anglo-Irish War of 1919–21.

One hundred and forty thousand Irish had fought in the federal (Union) armies in the Civil War (1861–5) with about half that number in the ranks of the Confederate forces. The wretched immigrants had at last discovered a country they could be patriotic about without ambivalence and they began to assume a conscious Irish-Americanism with its own culture and proud ethnic events such as the great St Patrick's Day parades. The growing entertainment business, especially in the vaudeville halls (which were very insistent about the clear green water between them and the shebeens and 'burlicues'), engendered writers and artists who had a clear perception of their audiences. 'Irish Molly-Os', 'Mother Machrees', 'Dacent Irish Boys' had to be catered for. And the songsmiths did the needful. (Most were not necessarily Irish and were as happy to please other ethnic groups. The Irish had only a brogue as a mark of difference; the Swedes, Germans, Bohemians and diaspora Jews had both to learn the language and lose the accent.) They wrote about Wild Irish Roses (from Tralee and elsewhere), Smiling Irish Eyes, with or without a tear, Old (decrepit, judged by the age of the singers) Irish Mothers, mud cabins and tumbledown shacks. They discovered 'A Little Bit of Irish in Sadie Cohen', wrote about 'My Yiddisha Colleen', asked Nora Malone to call them by phone, understood that 'Ireland Must Be Heaven for My Mother Came from There' and, to suit a not uncommon notion of the 'fightin'' Irish, dared people tread on the tail of their coats.

Emigration continued at a steady rate well into the 1920s and when in the 1930s films rather that music halls began to reflect the tastes and attitudes of the people, it was established that some gangsters, most priests, every cop and all girls with red hair and quick temper were Irish. The songs written by Edward Harrigan, Chauncey Olcott, George M. Cohan and others about 'Maggie Murphy's Home', 'Muldoon the Solid Man', 'Little Nelly Kelly', 'Me and Mamie O'Rourke' and 'A Little Bit of Heaven' recrossed the Atlantic to become more Irish than the Irish themselves.

This collection makes no apology for its vicarious nostalgia; the pieces are only a small selection from a vast store of Irish-Americana. Purists may writhe at the Oirishness of some of the entries but my Aunt Anna and your great-uncle Mick loved these songs and poems, used them as a badge of mixed nationality and by them paid their tribute to the green hills of (for them) a truly holy Ireland.

1

The Irish Emigrant

Whin I was a young man in th' ol' counthry, we heerd th' same story about all America. We used to set be th' tur-rf fire o' nights, kickin' our bare legs on th' flure an' wishing we was in New York, where all ye had to do was to hold your hat and the goold guineas'd dhrop into it. An' whin I got to be a man, I came over here with a ham and a bag iv oatmeal, as sure that I'd return in a year with money enough to dhrive me own ca-ar as I was that me name was Martin Dooley.

(Mr. Dooley: Chicago Evening Post, *17 July 1897)*

The Irish Emigrant

Lady Dufferin

One of the great emigrant songs written by the daughter of the Irish playwright Sheridan.

I'm sitting on the stile, Mary, where we sat side by
      side,
On a bright May morning long ago when first you
      were my bride.
The corn was springing fresh and green and the lark
      sang loud and high
And the red was on your lip, Mary, and the lovelight
      in your eye.
The place is little changed, Mary; the day is bright as
      then;
The lark's loud song is in my ear and the corn is green
      again
But I miss the soft clasp of your hand and your breath
      warm on my cheek,
And I still keep listening to the words you never more
      may speak –
You never more may speak.

I'm very lonely now, Mary, for the poor make no new
      friends
But, oh, they love the better still, the few the Father
      sends,
And you were all I had, Mary, my blessing and my
      pride.
There's nothing else to care for now, since my poor
      Mary died.
I'm bidding you a long farewell, my Mary kind and
      true,

But I'll not forget you, darlin', in the land I'm going
to.
They say there's bread and work for all and the sun
shines always there,
But I'll ne'er forget old Ireland, were it fifty times as
fair,
Were it fifty times as fair.

Teddy O'Neale

James Gaspard Maedar

Though written as a comic song in 1843 this is quite an elegant piece with a very plaintive tune. The belief that the Irish lived in 'cabins', accurate enough at the time this piece was written, lingered long after the post-Famine and Land-League reforms removed these from the Irish landscape.

I've come to the cabin he danced his wild jigs in,
As neat a mud cabin as ever was seen
And consid'rin' it served to keep poultry and pigs in
I'm sure it was always most elegant clean!
But now, all about it seems lonely and dreary,
All sad and all silent, no piper, no reel;
Not even the sun through the casement is cheery
Since I miss the dear darling boy, Teddy O'Neale.

I dreamt but last night (Oh bad luck to my dreaming;
I'd die if I thought 'twould come surely to pass)
But I dreamt while the tears down my pillow were
    streaming
That Teddy was courtin' another fair lass.
Och! did not I wake with a weeping and wailing,
The grief of that thought was too deep to conceal.
My mother cried, 'Norah, child, what is your ailing?'
And all I could utter was, 'Teddy O'Neale.'

Shall I ever forget when the big ship was ready
The moment had come when my love must depart.
How I sobbed like a spalpeen, 'Goodbye to you,
      Teddy.'
With drops on my cheek and a stone at my heart.
He says 'tis to better his fortune he's roving
But what would be gold to the joy I would feel
If I saw him come back to me, honest and loving,
Still poor, but my own darling Teddy O'Neale.

Anon

Typical broadsheet ballad of the 1850s, though with a romantic rather than an economic drive.

I'm bidding farewell to the land of my youth
    And the homes I love so well,
And the mountains so grand, in my own native land,
    I'm bidding them all farewell.
With an aching heart I'll bid them adieu
    For tomorrow I sail far away
O'er the raging foam, for to seek a home
    On the shores of Amerikay.

It's not for the want of employment I'm going;
    It's not for the love of fame,
That fortune bright, may shine over me
    And give me a glorious name.
It's not for the want of employment I'm going,
    O'er the weary and stormy sea,
But to seek a home for my own true love
    On the shores of Amerikay.

And when I'm bidding my last farewell,
    The tears like rain will blind,
To think of my friends in my own native land,
    And the home I am leaving behind.
But if I am to die on a foreign land
    And be buried so far far away,
No fond mother's tears will be shed o'er my grave
    On the shores of Amerikay.

The Moon Behind the Hill

William Kenneally

Originally called 'An Exile's Christmas Song' when it appeared in the Nation in 1856, this song was adopted by Edwin P. Christy (1815-62) for his black-face minstrel shows.

I watched last night the rising moon
    Upon a foreign strand,
Till mem'ries came like flowers of June
    Of home and fatherland:
I dreamt I was a child once more,
    Beside the rippling rill,
When first I saw in days of yore
    The moon behind the hill.

It brought me back the visions grand
    The purpled boyhood's dreams,
Its youthful loves, its happy land,
    As bright as morning beams;
It brought me back my own sweet Nore,
    The castle and the mill,
Until my eyes could see no more
    The moon behind the hill.

It brought me back a mother's love,
    Until, in accents wild,
I prayed her from her home above
    To guard her lonely child;
It brought me one across the wave
    To live in mem'ry still:
I brought me back my Kathleen's grave
    The moon behind the hill.

And there, beneath the silv'ry sky
   I lived life o'er again;
I counted all its hopes gone by
   I wept at all its pain;
And when I'm gone, oh! may some tongue
   The minstrel's wish fulfil
And still remember him who sang
   'The Moon Behind the Hill'.

Goodbye, Mursheen Durkin

Anon

Broadsheet ballad dating from soon after 1849 as the Gold Rush reference suggests.

In the days I went a courtin'
I was never tired resortin'
To the alehouse and the playhouse and many a house
      beside.
But I told my brother Séamus,
I'll be off now and grow famous
And before I come again, I'll roam the world wide.

Chorus (to be repeated after each verse)
So goodbye, Mursheen Durkin;
Sure, I'm sick and tired of workin'.
No more I'll dig the praties, no longer I'll be fooled:
But as sure as my name is Corney
I'll be off to Californy
And instead of diggin' praties, I'll be diggin' lumps of gold.

O! I courted girls in Blarney,
In Kanturk and Killarney,
In Passage and in Queenstown, I mean the Cove of
      Cork;
But I'm tired of all this pleasure,
So now I'll take my leisure,
And the next time that you hear, 'twill be a letter from
      New York.

Goodbye to all the boys at home;
I'm sailin' far across the foam
To try and make me fortune in far Amerikay.
There's gold and money plenty
For the poor and for the gentry
And when I come back again, I never more shall stray.

Ireland – A Seaside Portrait

John James Piatt

Poem by the American consul in Cork (1882–94) in com-
miseration with Erin and praise of the Statue of Liberty.

A great, still shape, alone
   She sits (her harp has fallen) on the sand,
And sees her children, one by one, depart –
Her cloak (that hides what sins besides her own!)
   Wrapped fold on fold about her. Lo
      She comforts her fierce heart,
As wailing some, and some gay-singing go,
With the far vision of that Greater Land
      Deep in the Atlantic skies,
      St. Brandan's Paradise!
      Another Woman there,
      Mighty and wondrous fair,
Stands on her shore-rock – one uplifted hand
      Holds a quick-piercing light
      That keeps long sea-ways bright;
She beckons with the other, saying, 'Come,
      O landless, shelterless,
Sharp-faced with hunger, worn with long distress –
      Come hither, finding home!
Lo, my new fields of harvest, open, free,
      By winds of blessing blown,
Whose golden corn-blades shake from sea to sea –
Fields without walls that all the people own!'

Off to Philadelphia

Anon

A ballad of emigration that contrives to be both plaintive and jaunty. A recording by John McCormack did justice to its energy.

My name is Paddy Leary,
From a shpot call'd Tipperary,
The hearts of all the girls I am a thorn in
But before the break of morn,
Faith! 'tis they'll be all forlorn
For I'm off to Philadelphia in the mornin'.

Chorus (to be repeated after each verse)
Wid my bundle on my shoulder,
Faith! there's no man could be boulder;
I'm lavin' dear ould Ireland widout warnin'
For I lately took the notion
For to cross the briny ocean
And I shtart for Philadelphia in the mornin'.

There's a girl called Kate Malone,
Whom I'd hoped to call my own,
And to see my little cabin floor adornin'
But my heart is sad and weary;
How can she be Missis Leary
If I shtart for Philadelphia in the mornin'!

When they told me I must lave the place
I tried to keep a cheerful face
For to show my heart's deep sorrow I was scornin'
But the tears will surely blind me
For the friends I have behind me
When I shtart for Philadelphia in the mornin'!

Extra Chorus
But tho' my bundle's on my shoulder
And there's no man could be boulder;
Tho' I'm lavin' now the shpot that I was born in.
Yet some day I'll take the notion
To come back across the ocean
To my home in dear ould Ireland in the mornin'!

The Old Bog Road

Teresa Brayton

*Effective and popular tear-jerker on both sides of the Atlantic
with text by an emigrant schoolteacher and a supporter of the
1916 Rising.*

My feet are here on Broadway this blessed harvest
          morn
But O the ache that's in them for the spot where I was
          born.
My weary hands are blistered from work in cold and
          heat
And O to swing a scythe today thro' fields of Irish
          wheat.
Had I the chance to wander back or owns a king's
          abode
'Tis soon I'd see the hawthorn tree by the old bog
          road.

When I was young and restless, my mind was ill at
          ease,
Though dreaming of America and gold beyond the
          seas.
O sorrow take their money, 'tis hard to get the same,
And what's the world to any man where no one speaks
          his name.
I've had my day and here I am with building bricks for
          for load,
A long three thousand miles away from the old bog
          road.

My mother died last springtide when Ireland's fields
      were green.
The neighbours said her waking was the finest ever
      seen.
There were snowdrops and primroses piled up beside
      her bed
And Ferns church was crowded when her funeral Mass
      was said.
But there was I on Broadway with building bricks for
      load,
When they carried out her coffin from the old bog
      road.

There was a decent girl at home who used to walk
      with me;
Her eyes were soft and sorrowful, like sunbeams on the
      sea.
Her name was Mary Dwyer but that was long ago
And ways of God are wiser that the things a man may
      know.
She died the year I left her, with building bricks for
      load.
I'd best forget the times we met on the old bog road.

Ah! life's a weary puzzle, past finding out by man;
I take the day for what it's worth and do the best I
      can.
Since no one cares a rush for me what needs to make a
      moan,
I go my way and draw my pay and smoke my pipe
      alone,
Each human heart must know the grief tho' little be its
      load;
So God be with you Ireland and the old bog road.

The Emigrant's Letter

Percy French

One of the most famous of French's sentimental songs, written in 1910, suggested by the overheard remark of a passenger.

Dear Danny, I'm takin' the pen in me hand
To tell you we're just out of sight of the land;
In the grand Allen liner we're sailin' in style
But we're sailin' away from the Emerald Isle;
And a long sort o' sigh seemed to rise from us all
As the waves hid the last bit of ould Donegal.
Och it's well to be you that is takin' your tay
Where they're cuttin' the corn in Creeslough the day.

I spoke to the captain – he won't turn her round
And if I swum back I'd be apt to be drowned.
I'll stay where I am, for the diet is great,
The best of combustibles piled on me plate,
But though it is 'sumpchus' I'd swop the whole lot
For the ould wooden spoon and the stirabout pot,
And Kitty forninst me a-wettin' the tay
Where they're cuttin' the corn in Creeslough the day.

There's a woman on board who knows Katey by sight
So we talked of old times till they put out the light.
I'm to meet the good woman tomorra' on deck
And we'll talk about Katey from this to Quebec.
I know I'm no match for her – oh! not the leesht
With her house and two cows and her brother a
                    preesht
But the woman declares Katey's heart's on the say
And mine's back with Katey in Creeslough the day.

If Katey is courted by Patsey or Mick,
Put a word in for me with a lump of a stick.
Don't kill Patsey outright – he had no sort of chance –
But Mickey's a rogue you might murther at wance;
For Katey might think, as the longer she waits,
A boy in the hand is worth two in the States:
And she'll promise to honour, to love and obey
Some robber that's roamin' round Creeslough the day.

Goodbye to you, Dan, there's no more to be said;
And I think the salt wather's got into me head,
For it dreeps from me eyes when I call to me mind
The friends and the colleen I've leavin' behind.
But still she might wait – whin I bid her goodbye,
There was just the last taste of a tear in her eye
And a break in her voice whin she said, 'You might
        stay,
But, plaze God, you'll come back to ould Creeslough
        some day.'

An Irish Mother

Percy French

Poem that became a song in 1962 when Brendan O'Dowda set it to music.

A wee slip drawin' water
    Me ould man at the plough.
No grown-up son nor daughter
    That's the way we're farmin' now.
'No work and little pleasure'
    Was the cry before they wint,
Now they're gettin' both full measure,
    So I ought to be contint.

Great wages men is givin'
    In that land beyant the say,
But 'tis lonely-lonely livin'
    Whin the childer is away.

Och, the baby in the cradle,
    Blue eyes and curlin' hair,
God knows I'd give a gra'dle
    To have little Pether here.
No doubt he'd find it funny
    Lyin' here upon me arm
Him – that's earnin' the good money
    On a Californy farm.

Six pounds it was or sivin
    He sint last quarter day,
But 'tis lonely-lonely livin'
    Whin the childher is away.

God is good – no better,
    And the Divil might be worse,
Each month there comes a letther
    Bringing somethin' for the purse.
An' me ould woman's heart rejoices
    Win I read they're doin' fine,
But it's oh! to hear their voices,
    And so to feel their hands in mine.

To see the cattle drivin'
    And the young ones makin' hay,
'Tis a lonely land to live in
    Whin the childher is away.

Whin the shadders do be fallin'
    On the ould man there an' me,
'Tis hard to keep from callin'
    'Come in, childher, to yer tea!'
I can almost hear them comin'
    Mary Kate and little Con –
Och! but I'm a foolish woman,
    Sure they're all grown up an' gone.

That our sins may be forgiven,
    And not wan go asthray,
I doubt I'd stay in Heaven
    If them childher was away.

Goodbye, Mick

Anon

Rather more cheerful emigration song with the old lie in the last verse.

Now the ship it sails in half an hour
    To cross the broad Atlantic
My friends are standing on the quay
    With grief and sorrow frantic.
I'm just about to sail away
    In the good ship *Dan O'Leary*.
The anchor's weighed and the gangway's up;
    I'm leaving Tipperary.

Chorus (to be repeated after each verse)
So goodbye, Mick, and goodbye, Pat,
    And goodbye, Kate and Mary.
The anchor's weighed and the gangway's up
    I'm leaving Tipperary.
And now the steam is blowing off;
    I have no more to say.
I'm bound for New York City, boys,
    Three thousand miles away.

In my portmantle here I have
    Some cabbage, greens and bacon
And if yez think I can't eat that
    It's there where ye're mistaken.
If the ship it plays at pitch and toss
    For half a dozen farthings,
I'll rowl my bundle on my back,
    And walk to Castle Gardens

Now won't I come the Yankee chat!
    I guess I'm calculatin'.
Come liquor up, old sonny boys,
    When an old friend is tratin'.
I'm as deep in love with Molly Burke
    As an ass is fond of clover.
When I get there I'll send for her;
    That's if she will come over.

A Little Bit of Heaven

'An' so 'twud go. Thin they had dinner, a hell iv a dinner, iv turkey or goose with bacon an' thin a bottle iv th' ol' shtuff with limon an' hot wather, an' toasts was drunk to th' la-ads far away an' to thim an' to another reunion, an' late at night me mother'd tuck us all in bed an' lade me father in his room with his jag upon him, singin' 'Th' Wearin' iv the Green' at th' top iv his voice. Thim ol' days!'

(Mr. Dooley: Chicago Evening Post, *23 December 1893)*

Kathleen Mavourneen

Julia Crawford

After the works of the perennially popular Tom Moore this is the greatest parlour ballad sung endlessly by sopranos both amateur and professional since its first appearance in 1837. The first line of the refrain has unfortunately caused the song's title to become a slang term for hire-purchase debt.

Kathleen Mavourneen, the grey dawn is breaking;
The horn of the hunter is heard on the hill;
The lark from her light wing the bright dew is
       shaking;
Kathleen Mavourneen, what slumbering still?
Oh has thou forgotten how soon we must sever?
Oh! hast thou forgotten this day we must part?

Chorus (to be repeated after each verse)
It may be for years and it may be forever.
Oh! why art thou silent, thou voice of my heart?
It may be for years and it may be forever.
Then why art thou silent, Kathleen Mavourneen?

Kathleen Mavourneen, awake from your slumbers;
The blue mountains glow in the sun's golden light.
Ah! where is the spell that once hung on my numbers?
Arise in thy beauty, thou star of my night.
Mavourneen, Mavourneen, my sad tears are falling,
To think that from Erin and thee I must part.

Killarney

Edmund Falconer

*Parlour favourite about the famous Kerry beautyspot popular
on both sides of the Atlantic, written by the Dublin playwright
Falconer for his play* Inishfallen *(1862) – the site of an
Augustinian monastery on the lower lake. The difficult words
'Heaven's reflex' at the end of each verse were later replaced by
the simpler 'Ever fair' and the word 'daff' in the third verse
means 'shake off'.*

By Killarney's lakes and fells,
Emerald isles and winding bays,
Mountain paths and woodland dells,
Memory ever fondly strays;
Bounteous nature loves all lands,
Beauty wanders ev'rywhere,
Footprints leaves on many strands
But her home is surely there;
Angels fold their wings and rest
In that Eden of the west,
Beauty's home, Killarney,
Heaven's reflex, Killarney.

Inishfallen's ruined shrine
May suggest a passing sigh;
But man's faith can ne'er decline
Such God's wonders floating by;
Castle Lough and Glena Bay:
Mountains Torc and Nagles' Nest,
Still at Muckross you must pray,
Tho' the monks are now at rest;
Angels wonder not that man
There would fain prolong life's span,

Beauty's home, Killarney,
Heaven's reflex, Killarney.

No place else can charm the eye
With such bright and varied tints;
Every rock that you pass by,
Verdure broiders or besprints;
Virgin there the green grass grows,
Ev'ry morn springs natal day,
Bright-hued berries daff the snows,
Smiling winter's frown away.
Angels often pausing there
Doubt if Eden were more fair,
Beauty's home, Killarney,
Heaven's reflex, Killarney.

Music there for Echo dwells,
Makes each sound a harmony;
Many-voiced the chorus swells
Till it faints in ecstasy;
With the charmful tints below,
Seems the heav'n above to vie:
All rich colours that we known,
Tinge the cloud wreath in the sky.
Wings of angels so might shine,
Glancing back soft light divine,
Beauty's home, Killarney,
Heaven's reflex, Killarney.

The Exile's Devotion

Thomas D'Arcy McGee

Ardent and romantic expression of patriotism by immigrant journalist.

If I forswear the art divine
    Which deifies the dead –
What comfort then can I call mine
    What solace seek instead?
For from my birth our country's fame
    Was life to me and love
And for each loyal Irish name
    Some garland still I wove.

I'd rather be the bird that sings
    Above the martyr's grave,
Than fold on fortune's cage my wings
    And feel my soul a slave;
I'd rather turn one simple verse
    True to the Gaelic ear,
Than sapphic odes I might rehearse
    With senates listening near.

O! Native Land, dost ever mark
    When the world's din is drown'd,
Betwixt the daylight and the dark
    A wandering solemn sound,
That on the western wind is borne
    Across they dewy breast?
It is the voice of those who mourn
    For thee, far in the West.

For them and theirs, I oft essay
  Your ancient art of song,
And often sadly turn away
  Deeming your rashness wrong;
For well I ween, a loving will
  Is all the art I own;
Ah me, could love suffice for skill
  What triumphs I had known!

My native land, my native land,
  Live in my memory still!
Break on my brain, ye surges grand!
  Stand up mist-covered hill!
Still in the mirror of the mind
  The land I love I see.
Would I could fly on the western wind,
  My native land, to thee.

Claribel [Charlotte Barnard, née Alington]

*Another parlour favourite popular on both sides of the Atlantic,
perhaps because the author was English and loaded with all the
Irish paraphernalia of its period (1866). [Mavourneen is an
anglicised form of the Irish* mo mhuirnín *(my little love),
Aroon* a rún *(darling).]*

Come back to Erin, Mavourneen, Mavourneen;
Come back, Aroon, to the land of my birth:
Come with the shamrocks and springtime, Mavourneen,
And it's Killarney shall ring with our mirth.

Sure when we lent you to beautiful England,
Little we thought of the long winter days,
Little we thought of the hush of the starshine
Over the mountains, the bluffs and the brays!

Chorus (to be repeated after each verse)
Then come back to Erin, Mavourneen, Mavourneen;
Come back, Aroon, to the land of my birth:
Come with the shamrocks and springtime, Mavourneen,
And its Killarney shall ring with our mirth.

O, but my heart sank when clouds came between us,
Like a grey curtain the rain falling down,
Hid from my sad eyes the path o'er the ocean
Far, far away where my Colleen has flown.

When by the fireside I watched the bright embers,
Then all my heart flies to England and thee,
Cravin' to know if my darlin' remembers,
Or if her thoughts may be crossin' to me.

The Exile's Return
(or, Morning on the Irish Coast)

John Locke

*The anthem of home-looking Irish–Americans written by a member of the IRB who died in exile. (*Th'anam an Dhia *is a sanctified version of* D'anam don diabhal = *Your soul to the devil, a mild expletive)*

Th'anam an Dhia but there it is -
    The dawn on the hills of Ireland!
God's angels lifting the night's black veil
    From the fair sweet face of my sireland!
O Ireland! isn't it grand you look –
    Like a bride in her rich adornin'
And with all the pent-up love of my heart
    I bid you the top of the mornin'.

This one short hour brings lavishly back
    For many a year of mourning;
I'd almost venture another flight,
    There's so much joy in returning –
Watching out for the hallowed shore
    All other attractions scornin'.
O Ireland! Don't you hear me shout?
    I bid you the top of the mornin'.

Ho, Ho! upon Cliodhna's shelving strand
    The surges are grandly beating
And Kerry is pushing her headlands out
    To give us kindly greeting;

Oh kind and generous Irish land,
  So real and fair and loving!
No wonder the wandering Celt should think
  And dream of you in his roving!

And doesn't old Cove look grand out there,
  Watching the wild waves motion,
Leaning her back up against the hills,
  And the tips of her toes in the ocean!
I wonder I don't hear Shandon's bells –
  Ah! maybe their chiming's over,
For it's many a year since I began
  The life of a Western rover.

For thirty summers, *asthore machree*,
  Those hills I now feast my eyes on
N'er met my vision save when they rose
  Over memory's dim horizon.
E'en so 'twas grand and fair they seemed
  In the landscape spread before me
But dreams are dreams, and my eyes would ope
  To see Texas sky still o'er me.

Oh! often upon the Texan plains
  When the day and the chase were over,
My thoughts would would fly o'er the weary wave
  And around this coastline hover;
And the prayer would rise that some future day –
  All danger and doubting scornin' –
I'd help to win for my native land
  The light of Young Liberty's mornin'.

Now fuller and clearer the coastline shows –
  Was ever a scene so splendid!
I feel the breath of the Munster breeze;
  Thank God that my exile's ended!
Old scenes, old songs, old friends again,
  The vale and the cot I was born in –
O Ireland! up from my heart of hearts
  I bid you the top of the mornin'!

Fred E. Weatherly

Of all the lyrics written for the most beautiful of Irish tunes, known (but not popularly) as 'The Londonderry Air', Weatherly's are the best known. Written in 1913 it was equally popular on both sides of the Atlantic and sung with like fervour by divas and drunks. The tune ascribed to the eighteenth-century Ruairí Dall Ó Catháin was taken down from a itinerant fiddler called McCormick at a fair in Limavady, County Derry by Jane Ross (1810–79) in 1851.

Oh Danny Boy, the pipes, the pipes are calling
From glen to glen and down the mountain side;
The summer's gone and all the roses falling,
It's you, it's you must go and I must bide.
But come ye back when summer's in the meadow
Or when the valley's hushed and white with snow;
It's I'll be here in sunshine or in shadow.
Oh Danny Boy, Oh Danny Boy, I love you so.

But when ye come, and all the flowers are dying,
If I am dead, as dead I well may be,
Ye'll come and find the place where I am lying
And kneel and say an *Ave* there for me;
And I shall hear, though soft you tread above me
And on my grave will warmer, sweeter be,
For you will bend and tell me that you love me
And I shall sleep in peace until you come to me.

I'll Take You Home Again, Kathleen

Thomas P. Westendorf

Song written in 1876 and extremely popular with Irish Americans though apart from the subject's name there's nothing Irish about it.

I'll take you home again, Kathleen,
Across the ocean, wild and wide,
To where your heart has ever been
Since first you were my bonny bride.
The roses all have left your cheeks;
I've watched them fade away and die;
Your voice is sad whene'er you speak
And tears bedim your loving eyes.

Chorus (to be repeated after each verse)
Oh! I will take you back, Kathleen,
To where your heart will feel no pain
And when the fields are fresh and green
I'll take you to your home again.

I know you love me, Kathleen dear,
Your heart was ever fond and true;
I always feel when you are near,
That life holds nothing dear but you.
The smiles that once you gave to me,
I scarcely ever see them now,
Tho' many, many times I see
A dark'ning shadow on your brow.

To that dear home across the sea
My Kathleen shall again return,
And when the old friends welcome thee,
Thy loving heart will cease to yearn.
Where laughs the little silver stream,
Beside your mother's humble cot
And brightest rays of sunshine gleam.
There all your grief will be forgot.

The Shamrock

Maurice Francis Egan

Poem by the child of pre–Famine immigrants who wrote many novels about the 'respectable' Irish and was Professor of English Literature at Notre Dame and the Catholic University of Washington.

When April rains make flowers bloom
   And Johnny-jump-ups come to light,
And clouds of color and perfume
   Float from the orchards pink and white,
I see my shamrock in the rain
   An emerald spray with raindrops set,
Like jewels on Spring's coronet,
   So fair, and yet it breathes of pain.

The shamrock on an older shore
   Sprang from a rich and sacred soil
Where saint and hero lived of yore
   And where their sons in sorrow toil;
And here, transplanted, it to me
   Seems weeping for the soil it left;
The diamonds that all others see
   Are tears drawn from its heart bereft.

When April rain makes flowers grow,
   And sparkles on their tiny buds
That in June nights will over-blow
   And fill the world with scented floods,
The lonely shamrock in our land –
   So fine among the clover leaves –
For the old springtime often grieves, –
   I feel its tears upon my hand.

Finley Peter Dunne

*Dunne's wonderful creation of Martin J. Dooley, the philosoph-
ical Irish saloon-keeper of Bridgeport, Chicago, was a successful
attempt to rescue the recently settled Irish from WASP derogation.
His subtle use of a dialect, partly American, partly Irish, made
the brogue respectable and showed its owners to be as clever, as
righteous and as patriotic as their racialist detractors. This
typical piece of Dooleyism, which appeared on 23 December
1893, was published, like the rest of his philosophical musings,
in the* Chicago Evening Post.

There was a turkey raffle on Halstead Street last night and
Mr. McKenna shook fifty-four. He came into Mr. Dooley's
with the turkey under his arm and Mr. Dooley, who was
mixing a Tom-and-Jerry dope on the end of the bar, paused
to inquire: 'Where'd ye get th' reed bur-rd, Jawnny?'

'I won it at Donnelly's raffle,' said Mr. McKenna.

'Ye ought to've kep' it in a warm place,' said Mr. Dooley.
'It's shrinkin' so 'twill be a fishball before ye get home. It
must be canned turkey. I've seen th'likes iv that in the ol'
counthry f'r ivrybody that cud get thim wanted turkey f'r
Chris'mas, an' if they cuddent get a big fat gobbler with
mate enough on him to feed a rig'ment iv Mayo min they
took what they got, an' they got wan iv them little herrin'
turkeys like the bur-rd ye've got under ye'er ar-rm. Faith,
it wasn't all iv thim wud get that much, poor things. There
was places in th' pa-art iv Ireland ye'er people come from,
Jawn, with ye'er di'mons an' ye'er gol'-headed umbrella,
where a piece iv bacon an' an exthra allowance iv pitaties
was a feast f'r th' kids. 'Twas in ye'er town, Jawn, that th'
little girl whin she wanted to remimber something, says to
th' ol' man: "Why," she says, "ye remimber 'twas th' day

they had mate," says she. She remimbered it because 'twas th' day they had mate, Jawn. 'Twas like Christmas an' th' Foorth iv July an' Pathrick's day, whin they had mate in ye'er part iv Ireland, Jawn. On other oc-casions they had pitaties an' butthermilk, or, if their neighbors wuz kind, oatmale stirabout. Poor things! Did I iver tell ye about me Uncle Clarence that died iv overatin' reed bur-rds?'

'You did,' said Mr. McKenna, surlily, for it was a point upon which Mr. Dooley often jibed him.

'Annyhow,' said Mr. Dooley, grinning, 'poor or rich alike, th'people iv Ireland never let th' Christmas pass without cellybratin'. Ye'd know th' day was comin' fr'm th' gr-reat coortin' that'd be goin'on iv'rywhere. Advint week was always a gr-reat coortin' time f'r th' la-ads. They'd make love before Christmas an' get married afftherward if th' gir-rls'd have thim an' they mostly would. That's a way th' gir-rls have the wide wur-rld over.

'Thin ivery man'd wish f'r a snowy Chris'mas. A green Chris'mas makes a fat graveyard, says th'good book, an' like as not there'd be snow on th' ground, at laste in Mayo where I come fr'm. An' about Christmas Eve th' lads and lasses'd go into th' hills an' fetch down ivy to hang above th' hearth an' all th' kids'd go light on the stirabout so's they could tuck in th' morrow. Christmas eve th' lads that'd been away'd come thrampin' in fr'm Gawd knows where, big lads far fr'm home in Cork an' Limerick an' th' City iv Dublin – come thrampin' home, stick in hand to ate their Christmas dinner with' th' ol' folks. Dear, oh dear, how I remimber it. 'Twas a long road that led up to our house an' me mother'd put a lamp in th' windy so's that th' la-ads could see th' way. Manny's th' time I've heerd th' beat iv th' stick on th' road an' th' tap on th' pane an' me mother runnin' to th' dure an' screamin', Mike, 'r Tim, 'r Robert Immit an' cryin'on his shoulder. 'Twas, let me see, four fours is sixteen, an' thirty makes forty-six –'twas in the Christmas iv fifty-sivin I last seen me brother Mike – poor fellow, poor fellow.

'We was up early ye may say that, th' nex' mornin'. Some iv the pious wans'd go to th' midnight mass an' thim we called "vo-teens". But th' kids had little thought iv mass 'til they opened their Christmas boxes. Poor little Christmas boxes they was like enough – a bit av a dolly f'r th' little girls an' a Jack-in-the-Box with whiskers like Postmaster Hesing's an' a stick iv candy. There's on'y wan thing ye have over here that we niver had at home, an' that's Sandy Claus. Why is it d'ye suppose? I never knew that St. Patrick druv him out with th' snakes, but I niver heerd iv him till I come to this counthry.

'Thin afther th' Christmas boxes th' kids'd go out in th' road an' holler 'Chrismas Box' at ivry man they met an' thin wud be off to mass where the priest's niece sung the "'Destah Fidelis", an' ivry man chipped in a shillin' or two f'r th' good man. By gar, some iv thim soggarths was bor-rn politicians, f'r they cud jolly a man f'r givin' big an' roast him f'r givin' little till ivry citizen in th' parish was thryin' to bate his neighbor like as if 'twas at a game av giveaway. Ye'd hear thim comin' home fr'm the church. "Th' iday iv Mike Casey givin' tin shillin's whin Badalia Casey borrid a pinch av tay fr'm me on'y las' week." "What a poor lot thim Dugans is. Before I'd be read fr'm th' altar with six pince after me name I'd sell th' shoes off me feet. I heard Tim Dugan got three poun' tin f'r that litter of boneens. Did you notice he went to his jooty to-day. Faith 'tis time. I was thinkin' he was goin' to join th' Prowtestants."

'An' so 'twud go. Thin they had dinner, a hell iv a dinner, iv turkey or goose with bacon an' thin a bottle iv th' ol' shtuff with limon an' hot wather, an' toasts was drunk to th' la-ads far away an' to thim an' to another reunion, an' late at night me mother'd tuck us all in bed an' lade me father in his room with his jag upon him, singin' 'Th' Wearin' iv the Green' at th' top iv his voice. Thim ol' days!'

'Well, Martin, good night,' said McKenna. 'A merry Christmas before I see you again.'

'Merry Christmas,' said Mr. Dooley. If Mr. McKenna

had returned five minutes later he would have found Mr. Dooley sitting on the edge of the bed in the back room wiping his eyes on the bar towel.

A Little Bit of Heaven
(Shure They Called It Ireland)

J. Keirn Brennan

Genuine Irish-American hit written in 1914, incorporated into the play The Heart of Paddy Whack *(1915) by Chauncey Olcott and sung regularly since. It was dedicated to Olcott's wife Rita.*

Have you ever heard the story of how Ireland got its
      name?
I'll tell you so you'll understand from whence old
      Ireland came.
No wonder that we're proud of that dear land across
      the sea,
For here's the way me dear old mother told the tale to
      me:

Chorus (to be repeated after each verse)
Shure, a little bit of heaven fell from out the sky one day
And nestled on the ocean in a spot so far away;
And when the angels found it, shure it looked so sweet
      and fair,
They said, 'Suppose we leave it, for it looks so peaceful
      there.'
So they sprinkled it with stardust just to make the
      shamrocks grow;
'Tis the only place you'll find them, no matter where you
      go.
Then they dotted it with silver to make its lakes so grand
And when they had it finished, shure they called it Ireland.

'Tis a dear old land of fairies and of wondrous wishing
        wells

And nowhere else on God's green earth have they such
        lakes and dells!

No wonder that the angels loved its shamrock-bordered
        shore,

'Tis a little bit of heaven and I love it more and more.'

Rida Johnson Young

Perhaps the most famous tear-jerker of all Irish-American songs, a typical product of an old and reliable partnership. Originally written in 1910 for an Irish entertainment called Barry of Ballymore, *it was recorded many times by John McCormack and became an unofficial signature tune. The lyricist worked with Victor Herbert, Jerome Kern and Rudolf Friml.*

There's a spot in me heart that no colleen may own;
There's a depth in me soul never sounded nor known;
There's a place in my mem'ry, my life, that you fill.
No other can take; nor one ever will.

Chorus (to be repeated after each verse)
Sure I love the dear silver that shines in your hair
And the brow that's all furrowed and wrinkled with care;
I kiss the dear fingers so toilworn for me
Oh, God bless you and keep you, Mother Machree.

Ev'ry sorrow or care in the dear days gone by,
Was made bright by the light of the smile in your eye;
Like a candle that's set in a window at night,
Your fond love has cheered me and guided me right.

Alice Furlong

Homegrown poem that could use an alternative title: 'The Judge's Dream of Home'. Dhrimmin (droimeann) *means 'whitebacked cow', fraughans are bilberries and gossoon* (garsún) *is a young boy.*

I'm a judge in Boston city, I've a countless hoard of
        dollars;
I go northward in the summer, I go southward in the
        snow.
I've the smartest fur-trimmed overcoats, the whitest
        linen collars,
I enjoy the best society with Presidents and scholars,
And the people shout, 'God bless him,' as I go.

The lawyers call me Solomon, the merchants call me
        Croesus:
I'm 'most affable' to journalists when I'm interviewed:
I can never pass the fashionable, photo-selling places,
But I'm smilingly confronted by my daughters' smiling
        faces;
They're exhibited in every attitude.

There's a queenly, quiet lady who is hostess at my table,
Who is mistress of my household, who is mother of
        my girls.
(Gentle wife!) she dresses finer than the princess in a
        fable,
Oh, the shimmer of her satin and the richness of her
        sable!
Oh, the glory of her diamonds and her pearls.

I have all that man can wish for, I am honou red and
        respected
By the highest and the lowest, by the freeman and the
        slave.
They put me down Vice-President for each new work
        projected,
For next session of the Congress I am sure to be
        elected –
Oh, my lost green land, my land beyond the wave!

Perhaps my eyes are age-dimmed, but I think that
        dawn was whiter
Over Connemara's mountains than behind that eastern
        range;
On the grey grass the young lark sang, with no human
        to affright her,
Yea, in Connemara's mountains even the song-bird's
        heart was lighter –
But in the strange land everything is strange.

I remember summer evenings, when my mother milked
        the *dhrimmin*
When the sun-rays on her white cap fell like rose-light
        on the snow,
How I thought the blue eyes like to Hers, the blessed
        amongst women,
And the red mouth bent and kissed me as the twilight
        gathered dim in
Cool recesses where the *fraughans* hide and grow.

Then we hurry through the gloaming lest the
        leprechaun belate us,
And the sheep-dog runs before us on quick-pattering,
        eager feet
For the father and the master and the supper all await
        us,
And no diamonds ever glistened like froth on the
        potatoes
In the three-legged skillet on the fire of peat.

Little silver flames go trembling through the blocks of
        glowing amber,
Reach the unlit outer edges, strain beyond ambitiously,
Rise like baby tides of moonlight, creep and fly and
        spring and clamber,
Lo! the firelight falls and flashes in the dusky, brown-
        roofed chamber –
And the gossoon laughs upon his father's knee!

Then I hear my mother whisper, 'Let us bless Him
        who has blessed us!'
And outside the corncrake murmurs in the depth of
        dewy grass,
In the dim blue sky the stars come out while we lie
        down and rest us –
I've been dreaming! here I'm sitting by my fire of stiff
        asbestos,
And my footman enters in to light the gas!

'Twas Only an Irishman's Dream

John J. O'Brien and Al Dubin

Song written in 1916 rehearsing an old, old theme.

I've roamed the wide world all over,
And of all the lands that I've seen,
There's no place I'd rather dwell in
Than the little Isle of Green.
Only last night I was gazing
On a sight that thrilled me thro',
For what I saw I'll see no more;
It was too good to be true.

Chorus (to be repeated after each verse)
Sure, the shamrocks were growing on Broadway,
*   Every girl was an Irish colleen*
And the town of New York was the county of Cork;
*   All the buildings were painted green;*
And the Hudson was just like the Shannon
*   Oh how good and real it did seem;*
I could hear mother singing,
*   Sweet Shandon bells ringing;*
'Twas only an Irishman's dream.

Ah, you never miss familiar scenes
Until you're far away;
Ah, you never know what homeland means
Until you're away to stay.
Then you picture each reminder
Of a face you sadly miss.
I'd give the world to dream again
Another dream like this.

3

When McGuiness Gets a Job

Do ye suppose there was anny wan sthruck f'r sympathy? Sare a wan. A gang iv Wexford min in th' nixt section come over an' offered half a day's wurruk an' th' Roscommon Lith'ry Society volunteered to fill th' places of the sthrikers with min that could handle a pick better thin any man fr'm wan ind iv Mayo to th' other.

(Mr Dooley: Chicago Evening Post, *14 September 1895)*

When McGuiness Gets a Job

Anon

Cry of an Irish-American wife, with proof of ethnic rivalry among nineteenth-Ocentury workers; the 'three-cornered box' is the hod for carrying bricks and mortar.

Last winter was a hard one, Mrs Riley, did you say?
Faith, myself it is that knows it for many a long day;
Your old man wasn't the only one who sat behind the
        wall;
There was my old man McGuiness didn't get a job at
        all.
The contractors they promised him that work on the
        boulevard
To handle the pick and shovel and throw dirt into the
        car;
Six weeks ago they promised him that work he'd surely
        get,
But believe me, my good woman, they're promising
        him yet.

Chorus (to be repeated after each verse)
Then cheer up, Mrs Riley, don't give way to the blues;
You and I will cut a shine with bonnets and new shoes,
And as for me, I've done a-sighing, no more I'll cry or sob
But I'll wait till times are better and McGuiness gets a job.

The Italians, devil take them, why don't they stay at
        home?
Sure we have enough of our sort to eat up all their
        own;
They come like bees in summer and in winter they go
        away,
The contractors hire hundreds for sixty cents a day;
They work upon the railroad, they shovel dirt and
        slush,
But there's one thing in their favor, Italians never lush;
They always bring their money home, they drink no
        beer or wine,
And that's something I would like to say about your
        old man and mine.

The spring time it is coming and soon we'll all get
        work,
McGuiness will go back to his trade, sure he's a
        handsome clerk;
You should see him climb the ladder, as nimble as a
        fox,
Faith he's the boy can juggle the old three-cornered
        box;
The boss he's always bawling, 'Hi there, don't you stop,
Keep your eyes upward, don't let no mortar drop.'
My old man is very careful, nothing he e'er lets fall
And damn the word you'd hear him say to my old man
        at all.

Drill, Ye Tarriers, Drill

Anon

Authentic sounding work song of Irish excavation workers who were called 'navvies' (navigators) when they dug Britain's canals. The song was sung (and spoken) by a Thomas Casey who had been a 'tarrier' briefly himself but the words and music are by that prodigious author Anon. Written in 1888 it was part of the repertoire of Maggie Cline who specialised in 'rough' barroom songs. The mention of the Staats Zeitung *is a reminder of the other large source of workers and national songs.*

Oh! ev'ry morn at seven o'clock
There are twenty tarriers on the rock;
The boss comes along and says, 'Be still
And put all your power in the cast-steel drill.
(*Spoken:* Stand out there with the flag, Sullivan. Stand back there! Blast! Fire! All over!)

Chorus (to repeated after each verse)
Then drill, ye tarriers, drill,
Drill, ye tarriers, drill.
Oh it's work all day without sugar in your tay
When ye work beyant on the railway,
And drill, ye tarriers, drill!

The boss was a fine man all around;
But he married a great big fat far-down;
She baked good bread and baked it well
And baked it hard as the hobs of H-ll.
(*Spoken:* Stand out forninst the fence with the flag, McCarthy. Stand back there! Blast! Fire! All over!)

The new foreman is Dan McCann,
I'll tell you he's a blame mean man,
Last week a premature blast went off
And a mile in the air went big Jim Goff.
(*Spoken:* Where's the fuse, McGinty? What he lit his pipe
with it! Stop the Belt car coming down. Stand back there!
Blast! Fire! All over!)

When payday next it came around
Poor Jim's pay's a dollar short he found.
'What for?' says he; then came this reply:
'You were docked for the time you were up in the sky.'
(*Spoken:* More oatmeal in the bucket, McCue. What's that
you're reading, Duffy, the *Staats Zeitung*?)

The Hod-Carrier's Song

Anon

Air: 'Villikens and His Dinah' (or as it is better known in Ireland, "Tis Six Miles from Bangor to Donaghadee').

I am a bold hodman; I live by my trade.
I mix up my mortar with my hoe and my spade,
And mount up the ladder, though ever so tall,
When the man of the trowel for mortar doth call.

Chorus (to be repeated after each verse)
Sing toor-al-li, toor-al-li, toor-al-lo-la.
Why don't you sing toor-al-li, toor-al-lo-la?

With my badge on my shoulder, fill'd with mortar or
   brick,
In my march up the ladder I'm nimble and quick;
With a heart light and cheerful, I whistle and sing,
Like a lark in the morning as she mounts on the wing.

As I stand on the scaffold with hod by my side,
I cast my eyes homeward o'er the deep rolling tide;
O'er the wide spread Atlantic to the land of my birth
More dear to my heart than any spot on this earth.

For there dwell the father and mother I love
And the maid I adore, my sweet turtle dove,
Whilst I, a poor hodman, an exile from home,
On freedom's fair shore a wanderer roam.

But a voice sweet I hear from the Emerald Isle
The voice of the maiden I left on the stile:
Be constant, dear Patrick, we'll soon meet again,
And that joy will reward us for all of our pain.

Yes, I hope soon to meet thee, fond maid of my heart,
And trust again that we never shall part;
At the thought of that meeting, my heart bounds with
      joy,
Where no vile intruder can our pleasures annoy.

Paddy on the Canal

Anon

The Paddies built many canals, beginning with the Erie which linked Lake Erie with New York via the Hudson River, its 363-mile length being completed on 25 October 1825.

When I landed in sweet Philadelphia, the weather was
        pleasant and clear,
I did not stay long in the city, so quickly I shall let
        you hear.
I did not stay long in the city, for it happened to be in
        the fall;
I never reefed a sail in my rigging, till I anchored out
        on the canal.

Chorus (to be repeated after each verse)
So fare you well father and mother
Likewise to only Ireland too;
So fare you well sister and brother
So kindly I'll bid you adieu.

When I came to this wonderful rampire, it filled me
        with the greatest surprise,
To see such a great undertaking, on the like I never
        opened my eye.
To see a full thousand brave fellows at work among
        mountains so tall,
To dig through the valleys so level, through rocks for
        to cut a canal.

I learned for to be very handy, to use both the shovel
      and spade,
I learnt the whole art of canalling; I think it an
      excellent trade.
I learned to be very handy, although I was not very
      tall,
I could handle the sprig of shillelagh with the best
      man on the canal.

The Boston Burglar

Anon

Famous criminal ballad of the 1840s.

I was born and bred in Boston –
It's a place you all know well –
Brought up by honest parents
The truth to you I'll tell.
Brought up by honest parents
And raised most tenderly
Till I became a sporting blade
At the age of twenty-three.

My character was taken
And I was sent to jail.
My parents tried to bail me out
But their efforts were in vain.
The jury found me guilty
And the clerk he wrote it down.
The judge he passed my sentence
And I was sent to Charlestown.

I can see my aged father
A-standing by the bar;
I can see my aged mother
A-pulling her grey hair,
A-pulling at her old grey locks
As the tears came tumbling down,
Saying, 'John, my son, what have you done
To be sent to Charlestown?'

4

Wakes and Weddings
and Every County Ball

An' ivry year comin' on Lint we had a ball in Finucane's hall
that ye'd never see th' like iv f'r fun and merriment. By hivins
they niver detailed liss than twinty polismen f'r it an' th' whole
foorce was on reserve whin it come off. Ho, ho, 'twas gorjous!
(Mr Dooley: Chicago Evening Post, *3 February 1894)*

Mick McGilligan's Ball

Michael Casey

Import from British music hall, more popular in Ireland and in America.

Michael McGilligan one fine day
Got a lot of money from the USA.
All through the death of his Uncle Joe
He got a million and a half or so.
Says McGilligan, 'I'll give a fancy ball
Down at the old ancestral hall,'
Invited neighbours ev'ryone
For to have some music and some rare old fun.

Chorus (to be prefixed as indicated after each verse)
(So they)
(And they)   All went down to Mick McGilligan's ball
(When they)
Where they had to tear the paper off the wall,
To make room for all the people in the hall
Oh, the girls and the boys made a divil of a noise
At Mick McGilligan's ball.

All of the neighbours came from near and far;
Mulligan arrived there in a motor car;
Old Missus O'Reilly, bless her heart,
Came with her family in a donkey-cart.
Pat O'Rafferty arrived in an aeroplane
And there was a shout when two old Skins
Came along at a gallop with two Miss Quinns.

Fluters and fiddlers danced around;
Drumming on the moleskin made a lovely sound;
They blew a gale on the old trombone,
Then reeled and rollicked to the piper's drone.
When they finished with the whiskey, beer and wine
They took a hand in 'Auld Lang Syne'.
There never was the like I do declare
Of that grand old hooley down in sweet Kildare.

If You're Irish Come into the Parlour

Shaun Glenville and Frank Miller

Song by one of the most famous pantomime 'dames'.

In sweet Lim'rick Town they say
Lived a chap named Patrick John Molloy.
Once he sailed to the USA
His luck in foreign parts he thought he'd try.
Now he's made his name and is a wealthy man;
He put a bit away for a rainy day.
So if you gaze upon the house of Patrick John
You'll find a notice that goes on to say:

Chorus (to be repeated after each verse)
If you're Irish come into the parlour;
There's a welcome there for you.
If your name is Timothy or Pat,
So long as you come from Ireland
There's a welcome on the mat.
If you come from the mountains of Mourne
Or Killarney's lakes so blue,
We'll sing you a song and we'll make a fuss;
Whoever you are you're one of us.
If you're Irish this is the place for you.

Patrick loved the girl he wed
But he could not stand his ma-in-law.
Once with joy he turned quite red
When she got into trouble with her jaw.
Six police they had to take her to the court.
She was informed a month she'd have to do;
So Patrick quickly wrote up to the judge a note
Explaining: 'Sir, I'm much obliged to you!'

The Maguires

Edward Harrigan

As sung in the comic play Squatter Sovereignty *(1881).*

Sure we're the boys from County Clare;
Oh, man alive, at wake or fair
No MacIntire wud ever dare
To face a darling, bold Maguire.
Wid hands as hard as marble stone,
We make our foes cry: 'Och, ochone!'
And send thim on a stretcher home,
The rarin', tearin', bold Maguires.

Chorus (to be repeated after each verse)
Faugh a ballagh, clear the way;
We're all alive at break o' day
Hail Columbi, 'Mericay
Oh, here's the darin', brave Maguires.

Oh, we're the faction that can drub
A MacIntire just like a spud
And walk on thim the same as mud
The rarin', tearin', bold Maguires.
Oh put us in an open lot;
We'd fight with bricks or cannon shot.
For ruction, boys, I'll tell ye what:
No one can bate the bold Maguires.

We never fear a friend or foe
But we give them blow for blow
And no white feather ever show
The rarin', tearin', bold Maguires.
We'd rather fight than ate a meal.
The MacIntires sure we can whale.
Now lock us up, we want no bail
The rarin', tearin', bold Maguires.

Lannigan's Ball

Anon

*Generic song (1863) about good fortune and resulting ruction,
native but quickly exported, which spawned many others.
Mavrone (*mo bhrón = *Alas! lit. my sorrow) and melia murder
(*míle murdar = *blue murder; lit. a thousand murders) confirm
its native origin. Chaney (verse 5) is vulgar Hiberno-English
for 'china'.*

In the town of Athy, one Jeremy Lannigan
Battered away till he hadn't a pound.
His father he died and made him a man again
Left him a farm and ten acres of ground.
He gave a grand ball to his friends and relations,
Who did not forget him when sent to the wall.
If you'll only listen I'll make your eyes glisten,
At the rows and the ructions at Lannigan's ball.

Myself, to be sure, got free invitation
For all the nice boys an' girls that I'd ask.
In less than a minute the friends and relations
Were dancing as merry as bees round a cask.
Miss O'Hara, the nice little milliner,
Tipp'd them a wink to give her a call
And soon we arrived with Timothy Galligan,
Just in time for Lannigan's ball.

They were doing all kinds of nonsensical polkas
All round the room in a neat whirligig
But Julia and me soon banished nonsense
And tipp'd them a twist of a real Irish jig.
Och, mavrone, 'twas she that was glad o' me
And danced till you'd think the ould ceiling would fall.
For I spent the whole fortnight at Burke's Academy,
Learnin' a step for Lannigan's ball.

The boys were all merry, the girls were all hearty,
Dancing away in couples and groups,
Till an accident happened young Terence McCarthy,
He put his right leg on Miss Flaherty's hoops.
The creature she fainted, roared milia murder,
Called for her friends and gathered them all;
Ned Carmody swore that he'd go no further
But he'd have satisfaction at Lannigan's ball.

In the midst of the row Miss Kerrigan fainted,
Her cheeks all the while being as red as the rose,
Some of the ladies declared she was painted,
She took a small drop too much, I suppose.
Her sweetheart, Ned Morgan, so powerful and able,
When he saw his fair colleen stretched by the wall
He tore the leg from under the table,
And smashed all the chaney at Lannigan's ball.

Oh, boys, there was a ruction,
Myself got a kick from big Phelim McHugh
But soon I replied to this kind introduction
And kicked up a terrible phillibooloo;
Ould Casey the piper was near being strangled,
They squeezed up his pipes, bellows, chanters and all;
The girls in their ribbons were all entangled,
And that put an end to Lannigans's ball.

Teaching McFadden to Waltz

Anon

Late nineteenth-century proof of social climbing which was imported into Ireland and claimed as homegrown.

Clarence McFadden he wanted to waltz
    But his feet weren't gaited that way;
So he saw a professor and stated his case
    And said he was willing to pay.
The professor looked in alarm at his feet
    And he viewed their enormous expanse
And he tacked on a five to his regular price
    For teaching McFadden to dance.

Chorus (to be repeated after each verse)
One, two, three, balance like me!
You're quite a fairy but you have your faults.
While your left foot is lazy, your right foot is crazy
But don't be unaisy: I'll teach you to waltz.

He took out McFadden before the whole class
    And showed him a step once or twice;
But McFadden his feet got tied in a knot;
    Sure he thought he was standing on ice.
At last he broke loose and struck out with a will,
    Never looking behind or before
But his head got so dizzy he fell on his face
    And chawed all the wax off the floor

McFadden soon got the step in his head
    But it wouldn't go into his feet.
He hummed 'La Gitana' from morning till night
    And he counted his steps in the street.

One night he went home to his room to retire
    After painting the town a bright red;
Sure he dreamt he was waltzing and let out his feet
    And kicked the dashboard off the bed.

When Clarence had practised his steps for a while
    Sure he thought he had it down fine.
He went to a girl and he asked her to dance
    And he wheeled her out into the line;
And he walked on her feet and he fractured her toes
    And said that her movement was false.
Sure, the poor girl went round for two weeks on a
        crutch
    For teaching McFadden to dance.

McCarthy's Party

Anon

One of the noisiest of party songs, popular since the turn of the century with students.

A nobleman you'll see, if you'll only look at me.
The other day I met McCarthy, walking down the way.
He to me did say: 'Won't you come down to our party?
Our house, to be sure, will be crowded to the dure.
Everyone will be gay and hearty.
The Murphys, Burkes and Baileys
Will be there with their shillelaghs.'
(Spoken) 'Where?'
'Down at McCarthy's party!'

Chorus (to be repeated after each verse)
At McCarthy's party everyone was hearty.
Someone hit Maloney on the nose.
With the handle of a broom
McCarthy swept the room.
Then a row arose; it was murder!
Murphy and his cousin paralysed a half-a-dozen;
They hit both swift and hard.
Now a number of the boys will never make a noise,
'Cause they're lying in the old churchyard.

Then began the row: I'll tell it to you now.
Burke you see was a bit of a dandy.
Maloney he got up, said he was a pup;
Told him straight that he wasn't worth candy.
Burke gave him a look, a frying-pan he took
To poor Maloney's nose
Gave him such a blatter, that shook him to his toes.
(Spoken) 'Where?'
'Down at McCarthy's party!'

A lady she did try for to pacify
My but she was a grand ould craytur!
Roaring like a bull, she was beautiful;
Madame Pether couldn't imitate her.
She opened her mouth, north, east, west and south
For all the world to see
She couldn't get it shut, so Murphy stuck his fut
(Spoken) 'Where?'
'Down at McCarthy's party!'

Anon

The ballad of an Irish-American brickie as he helped build New York. James Joyce used it as the title of his last work, the theme of indestructibility and resurrection suiting his theme of recirculation. The apostrophe was removed to become a cry to all the Finnegans in the coming times to rise again. The Irish phrase in the last line comes from the imprecation: 'D'anam do'n diabhal = lit. 'Your soul to the devil!'

Tim Finnegan lived in Walkin Street
A gentleman Irish mighty odd.
He had a tongue both rich and sweet
An' to rise in the world he carried a hod.
Now Tim had a sort of tipplin' way
With the love of the liquor he was born
An' to help him on with his work each day
He'd a drop of the craythur every morn.

Chorus (to be repeated after each verse)
Whack fol the dah, dance to your partner;
Welt the flure, yer trotters shake!
Wasn't it the truth I told you,
Lots of fun at Finnegan's wake.

One morning Tim was rather full;
His head felt heavy which made him shake.
He fell from the ladder and broke his skull;
So they carried him home his corpse to wake.
They rolled him up in a nice clean sheet
And laid him out upon the bed,
With a gallon of whiskey at his feet
And a barrel of porter at his head.

His friends assembled at the wake
And Mrs Finnegan called for lunch.
First they brought in tay and cake
Then pipes, tobacco and whiskey punch.
Mrs Biddy O'Brien began to cry,
'Such a neat clean corpse, did you ever see?
Arrah, Tim avourneen, why did you die?'
'Ah, hould your gab,' said Paddy McGee.

Then Peggy O'Connor took up the job.
'Biddy,' says she, 'you're wrong, I'm sure,'
But Biddy gave her a belt on the gob
And left her sprawling on the floor;
Oh then the war did soon engage;
'Twas woman to woman and man to man;
Shillelagh law was all the rage
An' a row and a ruction soon began.

Then Mickey Maloney raised his head
When a noggin of whiskey flew at him.
It missed and falling on the bed
The liquor scattered over Tim;
Bedad he revives! See how he rises
And Timothy rises from the bed
Says, 'Whirl your liquor round like blazes;
Thanam o'n dhoul, do you think I'm dead?'

Macnamara's Band

John J. Stamford

Comic song written in 1917 popular at home in Ireland but missing the inclusive Swedish verses. Ulysses S(impson) Grant (1822–1885), the successful Civil War general, was president 1868-1876. (Some versions have the Prince of Wales doing the handshaking.)

My name is Macnamara; I'm the leader of the band
And though we're small in number, we're the best in
      all the land.
Oh, I am the conductor and we often have to play
With all the best musicianers you hear about today.

Chorus (to be repeated after each verse)
Oh, the drums go bang and the cymbals clang
And the horns they blaze away;
McCarthy puffs the old bassoon, while Doyle the pipes
      does play;
Hennessy Tennessy tootles the flute and the music is
      something grand.
A credit to ould Ireland is Macnamara's band.

Whenever an election's on we play on either side –
The way we play our fine ould airs fills Irish hearts
      with pride.
Oh! if poor Tom Moore was living now, he'd make yez
      understand
That none could do him justice like ould Macnamara's
      band.

We play at wakes and weddings and at ev'ry county
ball

And at any great man's funeral we play the 'Dead
March' from *Saul*.

When General Grant to Ireland came he shook me by
the hand

And said he never heard the like of Macnamara's band.

Oh, my name is Uncle Yulius and from Sweden I have
come

To play with Macnamara's band and beat the big bass
drum,

And when I march along the street the ladies think I'm
grand.

They shout, 'There's Uncle Yulius playing with an Irish
band.'

Oh, I wear a bunch of shamrocks and a uniform of
green;

I'm the funniest looking Swede that you have ever
seen.

There's O'Briens and Ryans and Sheehans and
Meehans, they come from Ireland.

But by Yiminy I'm the only Swede in Macnamara's
band.

5

The Fighting Race

'Do you think there will be war?' Mr. McKenna asked.
'I don't know,' said Mr. Dooley. 'But if there is, I'm prepared
for to sacrifice th' last dhrop iv Hinnissy's blood an' th' last cint
iv Hinnissy's money before surrindhring.'
(Mr Dooley: Chicago Evening Post, 21 December 1895)

The Wearing of the Green

Dion Boucicault

*Boucicault's version of a broadside ballad of 1798 which he
featured in his popular play* Arrah-na-Pogue *(1864). The
third-verse compliment to the 'country beyond the sea' was
appreciated when it opened in New York the same year. The
word 'caubeen' in the second verse is an Irish word for 'hat'*
(cáibín).

O Paddy dear, and did you hear the news that's goin'
        round:
The Shamrock is forbid by law to grow on Irish
        ground;
St Patrick's Day no more we'll keep; his colours can't
        be seen,
For there's a bloody law against the wearing o' the
        green.
I met with Napper Tandy and he took me by the hand,
And he said, 'How's poor old Ireland and how does she
        stand?'
She's the most distressful country that ever yet was
        seen.
They are hanging men and women for the wearing of
        the green.

Then since the colour we must wear is England's cruel
      red,
Sure Ireland's sons will ne'er forget the blood that they
      have shed.
You may take the shamrock from your heart and cast it
      on the sod
But 'twill root and flourish there, though underfoot it's
      trod.
When law can stop the blades of grass from growing as
      they grow
And when the leaves in summertime their verdure dare
      not show,
Then I will change the colour that I wear in my
      caubeen
But till that day, please God, I'll stick to wearing of
      the green.

But if at last our colour should be torn from Ireland's
      heart
Her sons with shame and sorrow from the dear old isle
      will part;
I've heard a whisper of a country that lies beyond the
      sea
Where rich and poor stand equal in the light of
      freedom's day.
O Erin, must we leave you, driven by a tyrant's hand?
Must we ask a mother's blessing from a strange and
      distant land
Where the cruel cross of England shall nevermore be
      seen
And where, please God, we'll live and die still wearing
      of the green?

Thomas D'Arcy McGee

Necessary and salutary reminder to WASP America of Ireland's mythic/heroic past by an immigrant journalist who was assassinated later because of his denunciation of Fenianism.

Long, long ago, beyond the misty space
    Of twice a thousand years,
In Erin old there dwelt a mighty race,
    Taller than Roman spears;
Like oaks and towers they had a giant grace,
    Were fleet as deers,
With wind and waves they made their 'biding place,
    These western shepherd seers.

Their Ocean-God was Manannan Mac Lir,
    Whose angry lips,
In their white foam, full often would inter
    Whole fleets of ships;
Cromah their Day-God, and their Thunderer
    Made morning and eclipse:
Bride was their Queen of Song, and unto her
    They prayed with fire-touched lips.

Great were their deeds, their passions and their sports;
    With clay and stone
They piled on srath and shore those mystic forts,
    Not yet o'erthrown;
On cairn-crowned hills they held their council-courts;
    While youths alone,
With giant dogs, explored the elk resorts,
    And brought them down.

Of these was Finn, the father of the Bard
    Whose ancient song
Over the clamour of all change is heard,
    Sweet-voiced and strong.
Finn once o'ertook Grania, the golden-haired,
    The fleet and young;
From her the lovely, and from him the feared
    The primal poet sprang.

Ossian! two thousand years of mist and change
    Surround thy name –
Thy Fenian heroes now no longer range
    The hills of fame.
The very names of Finn and Gaul sound strange –
    Yet thine the same –
By miscalled lake and desecrated grange –
    Remains, and shall remain!

The Druid's altar and the Druid's creed
    We scarce can trace,
There is not left an undisputed deed
    Of all your race,
Save your majestic song, which hath the speed
    And strength and grace;
In that sole song, they live and love, and bleed –
    It bears them all through space.

O, inspired giant! shall we e'er behold,
    In our own time,
One fit to speak your spirit on the wold,
    Or seize your rhyme?
One pupil of the past, as mighty-souled
    As in the prime,
Were the fond, fair and beautiful, and bold –
    They of your song sublime.

'Private Myles O'Reilly'

*Comic piece by Charles Graham Halpine who, though his
sketches of military life were written as if by a private, rose to
the rank of brigadier in the 'Fighting 69th' in the Civil War
and enrolled the first black regiment for the Federal army. The
song deliberately confuses the name O'Ryan with the constellation
Orion.*

O'Ryan was a man of might
    Whin Ireland was a nation
But poachin' was his heart's delight
    And constant occupation.
He had an ould militia gun
    And sartin sure his aim was;
He gave the keepers many a run
    And wouldn't mind the game laws.

St Pathrick wanst was passin' by
    O'Ryan's little houldin'
And, as the saint felt wake and dhry,
    He thought he'd enther bould in.
'O'Ryan,' says the saint, 'avick!
    To praich at Thurles I'm goin'
So let me have a rasher quick
    And a dhrop of Innishowen.

'No rasher will I cook for you
    While better is to spare, sir,
But here's a jug of mountain dew
    And there's a rattlin' hare sir.'
St Pathrick he looked mighty sweet
    And says he, 'Good luck attind you,
And, when you're in your winding-sheet,
    It's up to heaven I'll sind you.'

O'Ryan gave his pipe a whiff –
    'Them tidings is transportin'
But may I ax your saintship if
    There's any kind of sportin'?'
St Pathrick said, 'A Lion's there,
    Two Bears, a Bull and Cancer.'
Bedad,' says Mick, 'the huntin's rare;
    St Pathrick, I'm your man, sir.'

So, to conclude my song aright,
    For fear I'd tire your patience,
You'll see O'Ryan every night
    Among the constellations.
And Venus follows in his track
    Till Mars grows jealous really
But faith, he fears the Irish knack
    Of handling the shillaly.

When Johnny Comes Marching Home

'Louis Lambert'

A song written in 1863 by the Irish-born Patrick Sarsfield Gilmore in the euphoria after Gettysburg and anticipating the end of the Brothers' War. It was based on the savagely satirical anonymous eighteenth-century Irish ballad, 'Johnny, I Hardly Knew You'. It was a tribute to the 140,000 Irish soldiers who fought in the Federal armies and became almost a second national song even in the South.

When Johnny comes marching home again, hurrah,
       hurrah,
We'll give him a hearty welcome then, hurrah, hurrah;
The men will cheer, the boys will shout,
The ladies, they will all come out.

Chorus (to be repeated after each verse)
And we'll all feel gay,
When Johnny comes marching home!

The old church bell will peal with joy, hurrah, hurrah,
To welcome home our darling boy, hurrah, hurrah;
The village lads and lassies say
With roses they will strew the way;

Get ready for the jubilee, hurrah, hurrah,
We'll give the hero three times three, hurrah, hurrah,
The laurel wreath is ready now,
To place upon his loyal brow;

Let love and friendship on that day, hurrah, hurrah,
Their choicest treasures then display, hurrah, hurrah;
And let each one perform some part
To fill with joy the warrior's heart.

The Croppy Boy *(A Ballad of 1798)*

'Carroll Malone'

Famous song by William McBurney who used the pen-name when he worked as a journalist on the Boston Pilot.

'Good men and true! in this house who dwell,
To a stranger bouchal, I pray you tell
Is the Priest at home? or may he be seen?
I would speak a word with Father Green.'

'The Priest's at home, boy, and may be seen;
'Tis easy speaking with Father Green;
But you must wait till I go and see
If the holy father alone may be.'

The youth has entered an empty hall –
What a lonely sound has his light foot-fall!
And the gloomy chamber's chill and bare,
With a vested priest in a lonely chair.

The youth has knelt to tell his sins;
'*Nomine Dei*,' the youth begins;
At '*mea culpa*' he beats his breast,
And in broken murmurs he speaks the rest.

'At the siege of Ross did my father fall
And at Gorey my loving brothers all,
I alone am left of my name and race,
I will go to Wexford and take their place.

'I cursed three times since last Easter day –
At mass-time once I went to play:
I passed the churchyard one day in haste,
And forgot to pray for my mother's rest.

'I bear no hate against living thing
But I love my country above my King.
Now Father! bless me and let me go
To die, if God has ordained it so.'

The priest said nought but a rustling noise
Made the youth look above in wild surprise:
The robes were off and in scarlet there
Sat a yeoman captain with fiery glare.

With fiery glare and fury hoarse,
Instead of a blessing, he breathed a curse –
"Twas a good thought boy to come here and shrive,
For one short hour is your time to live.

'Upon yon river three tenders float,
The priest's in one if he isn't shot
We hold his house for our Lord the King,
And, Amen, say, may all traitors swing!'

At Geneva Barrack that young man died,
And at Passage they have his body laid,
Good people who live in peace and joy,
Breathe a prayer and a tear for the Croppy Boy.

A Savage

John Boyle O'Reilly

A tribute from the leading nineteenth-century Irish-American poet to a member of another minority. He himself avoided execution for Fenianism on commutation and escaped from penal servitude to become part-owner of the Boston Pilot.

Dixon, a Choctaw, twenty years of age,
    Had killed a miner in a Leadville brawl;
Tried and condemned, the rough-beards curb their rage
    And watch him stride in freedom from the hall.

'Return on Friday, to be shot to death!'
    So ran the sentence, – it was Monday night.
The dead man's comrades drew a well-pleased breath;
    Then all night long the gambling-dens were bright.

The days sped slowly; but the Friday came,
    And flocked the miners to the shooting-ground;
They choose six riflemen of deadly aim,
    And with low voices sat and lounged around.

'He will not come.' 'He's not a fool.' 'The men
    Who set the savage free must face the blame.'
A Choctaw brave smiled bitterly, and then
    Smiled proudly, with raised head, as Dixon came.

Silent and stern, a woman at his heels,
    He motions to the brave, who stays her tread.
Next minute flame the guns, – the woman reels
    And drops without a moan: Dixon is dead.

The Fighting Race

Joseph Ignatius Constantine Clarke

Clarke's poem was based upon his own experiences as a reporter in the Spanish-American War of 1898. Marye's Heights was one of the battles of the Civil War (1861-5) and the engagements referred to by Shea in the fourth verse mainly involved soldiers of the Irish Brigade who fought in eighteenth-century Europe.

'Read out the names,' and Burke sat back
And Kelly droop'd his head,
While Shea – they call'd him 'Scholar Jack' –
Went down the list of the dead,
Of the officers, seamen, gunners, marines,
The crews of the gig and yawl,
The bearded man and the lad in his teens,
The carpenters, coalpressers, all;
Then knocking the ashes from out his pipe
Said Burke, in an off-hand way,
'We're in the dead man's list, by cripe!
Kelly and Burke and Shea.'
'Well here's to the Maine, and I'm sorry for Spain,'
Said Kelly and Burke and Shea.

'Where there's Kellys there's trouble,' says Burke,
'Wherever fighting's the game
Or spice of danger in grown man's work,'
Said Kelly, 'you'll find my name.'
'And do we fall short,' says Burke getting mad,
'When it's touch and go for life?'
Said Shea, 'It's thirty odd years, bedad,
Since I charg'd to drum and fife
Up Marye's Heights and my old canteen
Stopped a rebel ball on its way;

There were blossoms of blood on our sprigs of green –
Kelly and Burke and Shea –
And the dead didn't brag.' 'Well, here's to the flag!'
Said Kelly and Burke and Shea.

I wish 'twas in Ireland, for there's the place,'
Said Burke, 'that we'd die by right
In the cradle of our soldier race
After one good stand-up fight;
My grandfather fell at Vinegar Hill
And fighting was not his trade;
But his rusty pike's in the cabin still
With Hessian blood on the blade.'
'Aye, aye,' said Kelly, 'the pikes were great
When the word was "Clear the way!",
We were thick on the roll in Ninety-Eight,
Kelly and Burke and Shea.'
'Well, here's to the pike and the sword and the like!'
Said Kelly and Burke and Shea.

And Shea, the scholar, with rising joy,
Said, 'We were at Ramillies;
We left our bones at Fontenoy
And up in the Pyrenees;
Before Dunkirk, on Landen's plain,
Cremona, Lille and Ghent.
We're all over Austria, France and Spain
Wherever they pitched a tent.
We died for England from Waterloo
To Egypt and Dargai;
And still there's enough for a corps or two,
Kelly and Burke and Shea.'
'Well here's to good honest fighting blood!'
Said Kelly and Burke and Shea.

'Oh, the fighting races don't die out,
If they seldom die in their bed,
For love is first in their hearts, no doubt.'
Said Burke; then Kelly said:
'When Michael, the Irish archangel, stands,
The angel with the sword,
And the battle-dead from a hundred lands
Are ranged in one big horde,
Our line, that for Gabriel's trumpet waits,
Will stretch three deep that day –
From Jehoshaphat to the Golden Gates
Kelly and Burke and Shea.'
'Well, here's thanks to God for the race and the sod!'
Said Kelly and Burke and Shea.

The General's Death

Joseph O'Connor

Elegy (probably on General Sedgewick who was killed at Spotsylvania in 1864) by a second-generation Irish journalist whose poet brother Michael was killed at the Potomac in 1862.

The general dashed along the road
　　Amid the pelting rain;
How joyously his bold face glowed
　　To hear our cheers refrain!

His blue blouse flapped in wind and wet
　　His boots were splashed with mire,
But round his lips a smile was set,
　　And in his eyes a fire.

A laughing word, a gesture kind, _
　　We did not ask for more,
With thirty weary miles behind,
　　A weary fight before.

The gun grew light to every man,
　　The crossed belts ceased their stress,
As onward to the column's van
　　We watched our leader press.

Within an hour we saw him lie,
　　A bullet in his brain,
His manly face turned to the sky,
　　And beaten by the rain.

The Fenian Man-O'-War

Anon

Ballad of 1867 when the Jacknell Packet, *a two-hundred ton brig, renamed* Erin's Hope, *was used by the Fenian Brotherhood to run arms to Ireland which in fact were never landed.*

'Twas down by Boston Harbour I carelessly did stray;
I overheard a sailor lad these words to his love say:
'O Bridget, dearest Bridget, from you I must go far
To fight against the cruel foe on the Fenian Man O'-
      War.'

'O Patrick, dearest Patrick, don't go away from me;
For the foeman they are treacherous as ever they can
      be
And by some cruel dagger you might receive a scar.
O Patrick dear, don't venture near the Fenian Man-O'-
      War.'

They both sat down together; then they rose to stand.
A Fenian crew surrounded him and rowed him from
      the land.
Then Patrick raised a Fenian flag and waved it near
      and far
And Bridget blessed her sailor boy on board the Man-
      O'-War.

Anon

Song popular in America just after the Civil War when the Irish Republican Brotherhood recruited trained Irish military personnel for anti-British activity. It was used as a Fenian recruiting song.

Will you come to the bower o'er the free boundless
   ocean,
Where the stupendous waves roll in thundering motion,
Where the mermaids are seen and the fierce tempest
   gathers
To loved Erin the green, the dear land of our fathers.

Chorus (to be repeated after each verse)
Will you come, will you, will you come to the bower?

Will you come to the land of O'Neill and O'Donnell,
Of Lord Lucan of old and immortal O'Connell,
Where Brian drove the Danes and St Patrick the
   vermin
And whose valleys remain still most beautiful and
   charming.

You can visit Benburb and the storied Blackwater
Where Owen Roe met Munro and his chieftains did
   slaughter,
Where lambs skip and play on the mosyall over
From those bright golden views to enchanting
   Rostrevor.

You can see Dublin city and the fine groves of Blarney,
The Bann, Boyne and Liffey, and the lakes of
      Killarney;
You may ride on the tide on the broad majestic
      Shannon;
You may sail round Lough Neagh and see storied
      Dungannon.

You can visit New Ross, gallant Wexford and Gorey,
Where the green was last seen by proud Saxon and
      Tory,
Where the soil is sanctified by the blood of each true
      man,
Where they died satisfied that their enemies they
      would not run from.

Will you come and awake our lost land from its
      slumber
And her fetters we'll break, links that long are
      encumbered
And the air will resound with hosannahs to greet you;
On the shore will be found gallant Irishmen to greet
      you.

Mush, Mush

Anon

*Mid-nineteenth-century song popular with college students
and showing signs of its 'for export' intentions in the overdone
(and imperfect) phonetic rendering of Munster pronunciation.
This version I found in a Scottish students' songbook of the
1890s.*

Oh, 'twas there I larned readin' and writin',
At Bill Bracket's where I went to school
And 'twas there I larned howlin' an' fightin'
With my schoolmaster Misther O'Toole.
Him an' me had many a scrimmage
And the divil a copy I wrote.
There was ne'er a gossoon in the village
Dared thread on the tail o' me . . .

Chorus (to be repeated after each verse)
Mush, mush too-ral-i-aday
Mush, mush too-ral-i-ay
There was ne'er a gossoon in the village
Dared thread on the tail o' me coat.

Oh 'twas there that I learned all me courtin'
Many lessons I tuck in the art
Till Cupid, the blackguard, in sportin'
An arrow dhruv straight thro' my heart.
Miss Judy O'Connor, she lived jist forninst me
An' tinder lines to her I wrote.
If ye dare say a hard word agin her
I'll thread on the tail o' yer...

But a blackguard called Mickey Maloney
Came an' sthole her affictions away;
Fir he'd money an' I hadn't any
So I sint him a challenge nixt day.
In the ayvenin' we met by the Woodbine;
The Shannon we crossed in a boat;
An' I lathered him wid me shillaly
For he throd on the tail o' me...

Oh, me fame wint abroad thro' the nation
An' folks came a-flockin' to see;
An' they cried out widout hesitation:
'You're a fightin' man, Billy McGee.
I've cleaned out the Finnegan faction
An' I've licked all the Murphys afloat;
If your in fur a row or a ruction
Jist thread on the tail o' me...

John W. Kelly

A song featured by Maggie Cline, the 230lb star of Irish-American vaudeville. She bought it in 1890 from the author who was known as 'The Rolling-Mill Man' for two dollars, and it and 'Drill, Ye Tarriers' (see p. 65) were her stock in trade for years in the 1890s. The song with its information about contemporary pugilism and racial insights is the kind beloved of sociologists.

'Twas down at Dan McDevitt's at the corner of this
        street;
There was to be a prizefight and both parties were to
        meet
To make all the arrangements and see everything was
        right.
McCloskey and a nagur were to have a finish fight.
The rules were London Prize Ring and McCloskey
        said he'd try
To bate the nagur with one punch or in the ring he'd
        die.
The odds were on McCloskey tho' the betting it was
        small;
'Twas on McCloskey ten to one, on the nagur none at
        all.

Chorus (to be repeated after each verse)
'Throw him down McCloskey,' was to be the battle cry.
'Throw him down McCloskey, you can lick him if you try,'
And future generations with wonder and delight
Will read on hist'ry's pages of the great McCloskey fight.

The fighters were to start in at a quarter after eight
But the nagur did not show up and the hour was
        getting late.
He sent around a messenger who then went on to say
That the Irish crowd would jump him and he wouldn't
        get fair play.
Then up steps Pete McCracken and said that he would
        fight
Stand-up or Rough and Tumble if McCloskey didn't
        bite.
McCloskey says, 'I'll go you,' then the seconds got in
        place
And the fighters started in to decorate each other's
        face.

They fought like two hyenas till the forty-second
        round.
They scattered blood enough around, by gosh, to paint
        the town.
McCloskey got a mouthful of poor McCracken's jowl;
McCracken hollered, 'Murthur!' and the seconds
        hollered, 'Foul'.
The friends of both the fighters that instant did begin
To fight and ate each other; the whole party started in,
You couldn't tell the difference in the fighters if you'd
        try:
McCracken lost his upper lip; McCloskey lost an eye.

A Challenge

John L(awrence) Sullivan (1858–1918)

This letter appeared in all the sporting pages in America on 23 March 1882 from Sullivan who from 1882 until 1892 completely dominated the US prize ring, until his defeat by another Irish-American, 'Gentleman Jim' Corbett (1866–1933), in the 21st round.

There has been so much newspaper talk from parties who state that they are desirous of meeting me in the ring that I am disgusted. Nevertheless, I am willing to fight any man in this country, for five thousand dollars a side: or, any man in the old country for the same amount at two months from signing articles, – I use gloves, and he, if he pleases, to fight with the bare knuckles. I will not fight again with the bare knuckles, as I do not wish to put myself in a position amenable to the law. My money is always ready, so I want these fellows to put up or shut up.

John L. Sullivan

Clancy Lowered the Boom

Anon

'Fighting Irish' song from the days before universal household refrigeration.

Now Clancy was a peaceful man if you know what I
       mean;
The cops picked up the pieces after Clancy left the
       scene.
He never looked for trouble; that's a fact you can
       assume
But nevertheless when trouble would press
Clancy lowered the boom!

Chorus (to be repeated after each verse)
Oh, that Clancy, Oh, that Clancy!
Whenever they got his Irish up
Clancy lowered the boom!

O'Leary was a fighting man; they all knew he was tough.
He strutted 'round the neighbourhood a-shooting off
       the guff.
He picked a fight with Clancy; then and there he
       sealed his doom.
Before you could shout, 'O'Leary, look out!'
Clancy lowered the boom!

O'Houlihan delivered ice to Mrs Clancy's flat.
He'd always linger for a while to talk of this and that.
One day he kissed her just as Clancy walked into the
       room
Before you could say the time of day
Clancy lowered the boom!

6

My Irish Molly, O

'Was ye iver in love, Jawn?' said Mr Dooley. 'I sup-pose ye was – before ye was marrid?'

'Yes,' said Mr. McKenna. 'And why?'

'Nawthin',' said Mr. Dooley. 'On'y I was thinkin' 'tis a damn quare disease. I had it wanst mesilf, but 'tis so long ago that I near forgot it. I sup-pose I had it bad, too, as anny wan.'

(*Mr Dooley:* Chicago Evening Post, 5 May 1894)

Samuel Lover

An import from home by the novelist, painter and entertainer who was the grandfather of Victor Herbert (1859–1924), the composer of many Broadway hits. It was written in 1841 for a broad skit on Italian opera Il Paddy Whack in Italia. *The word bawn comes from* bán *(fair-haired).*

Oh! Molly Bawn, why leave me pining,
All lonely waiting her for you,
While the stars above are brightly shining
Because they've nothing else to do.
(Repeated as chorus)

The flowers, late, were open keeping,
To try a rival blush with you.
But their mother, Nature, set them sleeping
With their rosy faces wash'd with dew.

Now the pretty flow'rs were made to bloom dear,
And the pretty stars were made to shine;
And the pretty girls were made for the boys, dear,
And maybe you were made for mine.

The wicked watchdog here is snarling.
He takes me for a thief you see,
For he knows I'd steal you, Molly darling
And then transported I should be.

Molly Brallaghan

Anon

Comic song of the early nineteenth century, an Irish emigrant that made good in America. 'Wirra' in the second line is from the Gaelic A Mhuire = O (Virgin) Mary. A salamander (last verse) was a redhot poker used for kindling.

Och man dear, did you ever hear of purty Molly
      Brallaghan?
Ah, wirra, there she's left me and I'll never be a man
      again;
There's not another summer's sun will e'er my poor
      hide tan again,
Since Molly, she has left me all alone for to die.
The place where my poor heart was, you'd aisy roll a
      turnip in,
'Tis the size of all Dublin from the city to the Devil's
      Glen.
If she car'd to take another sure she might have sent
      mine back again
And not have left me by myself alone for to die.

Och man dear, I remember when the milking time was
      past and gone;
We went into the meadows where she swore I was the
      only one
That ever she could love; yet, oh the base and cruel
      one,
After that to leave me all alone for to die.
Och man dear, I remember as we came home the rain
      began
And I rolled her in my frieze coat, tho' ne'er a
      waistcoat I had on.

My shirt was rather fine drawn and oh! the base and
        cruel one,
After that to leave me all alone for to die.

I went and told my tale to Father McDonnell, man.
He bid me for to ax advice of Counsellor McConnell,
        man,
Who told me promise breaches had been ever since the
        world began,
Now I'd only got one pair, man, and they're corduroy.
Och, man, now what could he mean? or what would
        you advise me to?
Must my corduroys to Molly go? In troth I'm bothered
        what to do.
I can't afford to lose my heart and then to lose my
        breeches too.
Yet what need I be caring, when I've only to die.

The left side of my carcase is as weak as water gruel,
        man,
And nothing's left upon my bones, since Molly's been
        so cruel, man.
I wish I had a blunderbuss; I'd go and fight a duel,
        man.
It's better for to kill myself than stay here to die.
I'm hot and I'm determined, as any 'Salamander' man
Won't you come to my wake, when I go my long
        meander, man.
I'll feel as valiant as the famous Alexander, man.
When I hear you crying round me: 'Arrah, why did you
        die?'

Colleen Dhas Cruthen na Moe
(Cailín Deas Crúite na mBó
= *Pretty Milkmaid)*

Anon

The original sheet music says correctly that the tune is an ancient Irish melody and the first version is by Alexander Lee. This second was written by Dion Boucicault for his play The Colleen Bawn *(1860) and later used by George M. Cohan in his Broadway show* Little Nelly Kelly *(1922).*

It was on a fine summer's morning;
The birds sweetly tuned on each bow
And as I walk'd out for my pleasure
I saw a maid milking her cow.
Her voice so enchanting melodious
Left me quite unable to go;
My heart it was loaded with sorrow
For Colleen dhas crutha na moe.

Then to her I made my advances
'Good morrow, most beautiful maid!
Your beauty my heart so entrances.'
'Pray, Sir, so not banter!' she said.
'I'm not such a rare a precious Jewel
That I shall enamour you so;
I am but a poor little milk girl,'
Says Colleen dhas crutheen na moe.

The Indies afford no such Jewel
So bright and transparently clear;
Ah! do not add flame to my fuel;
Consent but to love me, my dear.
Ah! had I the lamp of Aladdin
Or the wealth of the African shore,
I would rather be poor in a cottage
With Colleen dhas crutheen na moe.

'Twas on a bright morning in summer
I first heard his voice speaking low,
As he said to a colleen beside me,
'Who's that pretty girl milking her cow?'
And many times after he met me,
And vow'd that I always should be
His own little darling alanna
Mavourneen a sweelish machree.

I haven't the manner or graces
Of the girls in the world where ye move;
I haven't their beautiful faces
But I have a heart that can love.
If it please ye, I'll dress in satins
And jewels I'll put on my brow
But don't ye be after forgettin'
Your pretty girl milking her cow.

The Rose of Tralee

William Pembroke Mulchinock

One of the most popular of the Irish immigrants brought from his native Kerry by the author in 1849. The poem was written for a Catholic servant Mary O'Connor, with whom Mulchinock fell in love and who soon afterwards died of tuberculosis.

The pale moon was rising above the green mountain,
The sun was declining beneath the blue sea,
When I strayed with my love to the pure crystal
        fountain
That stands in the beautiful vale of Tralee.
She was lovely and fair as the rose of the summer;
Yet 'twas not her beauty alone that won me.
Oh, no! 'twas the truth in her eye ever dawning
That made me love Mary, the Rose of Tralee.

The cool shades of evening their mantle were spreading
And Mary all-smiling was list'ning to me
The moon thro' the valley its pale rays was shedding
When I won the heart of the Rose of Tralee.
Though lovely and fair as the rose of the summer;
Yet 'twas not her beauty alone that won me.
Oh, no! 'twas the truth in her eye ever dawning
That made me love Mary, the Rose of Tralee.

Johnny Patterson

'Positive' emigration sung written by 'The Irish Clown' in 1882 for one of his Stateside tours. The picture of the bird (last verse) is that on the dollar.

It was in the County Kerry,
    A little way from Clare,
Where the boys and girls are merry
    At pattern, race or fair;
The town is called Killorglin,
    A pretty place to view
But what makes it interesting
    Is my Bridget Donahue.

Chorus (to be repeated after each verse)
Oh, Bridget Donahue,
I really do love you;
Although I'm in America,
To you I will be true.
Then, Bridget Donahue,
I'll tell you what I'll do:
Just take the name of Patterson
And I'll take Donahue.

Her father is a farmer;
    A dacent man is he;
He's liked by all the people
    From Killorglin to Tralee,
And Bridget, on a Sunday
    When coming home from Mass,
She's admired by all the people;
    Sure they wait to see her pass!

I sent her home a picture;
    I did upon my word;
Not a picture of myself
    But just a picture of a bird.
It was the Yankee eagle.
    Says I: 'Miss Donahue,
Our eagle's wings are large enough
    To shelter me and you.'

My Wild Irish Rose

Chauncey Olcott

A song written in 1899 that rivalled 'When Irish Eyes Are Smiling' for popularity with bar-room and other tenors. The title was suggested to Olcott on his single visit to Ireland when, it is said, in order to stop a Killarney boy from singing seann-nós Gaelic songs he asked him the name of a flower growing by Lough Lene and he answered, 'Tis just a wild Irish rose.'

If you listen I'll sing you a sweet little song
Of a flower that's now drooped and dead.
Yet dearer to me than all of its mates,
Tho' each holds aloft its sweet head.
'Twas given to me by a girl that I know,
Since we met, faith, I've known no repose.
She is dearer by far than the world's brightest star,
And I call her my wild Irish Rose.

Chorus (to be repeated after each verse)
My wild Irish Rose, the sweetest flower that grows;
You may search ev'rywhere but none can compare
With my wild Irish Rose.
My wild Irish Rose, the dearest flower that grows;
And someday for my sake, she may let me take
The bloom from my wild Irish Rose.

They may think of their roses, which by other names,
Would smell just as sweetly they say;
But I know that my Rose would never consent
To have that sweet name taken away.
Her glances are shy whene'er I pass by
The bower where my true love grows
And my one wish has been that some day I may win
The heart of my wild Irish Rose.

Little Annie Rooney

Michael Nolan

Song performed by the author, very popular with the London Irish and pirated by the American publishers. Its waltztime chorus made it the bestselling sheetmusic of 1889.

A winning way, a pleasant smile,
Dressed so neat but quite in style,
Merry chaff your time to wile,
Has little Annie Rooney.
Ev'ry evening, rain or shine,
I make a call twixt eight and nine,
On her who shortly will be mine,
Little Annie Rooney.

Chorus (to be repeated after each verse)
She's my sweetheart, I'm her beau
She's my Annie; I'm her Joe
Soon we'll marry,
Never – to part
Little Annie Rooney
Is my sweetheart.

The parlour's small but neat and clean
And set with taste so seldom seen,
And you can bet, the household queen
Is little Annie Rooney.
The fire burns cheerfully and bright,
As a family circle round each night,
We form, and ev'ry one's delight
Is little Annie Rooney

We've been engaged close on a year;
The happy time is drawing near.
I'll wed the one I love so dear,
Little Annie Rooney.
My friends declare I'm in a jest,
Until the time comes will not rest,
But one who knows its value best
Is little Annie Rooney

Macushla

Josephine V. Rowe

One of John McCormack's 'finishers' written in 1910 to which, as with 'Mother Machree', he gave some concert platform respectability. The title is a transliteration of the Gaelic mo chuisle *(my beloved, lit: my pulse) and the lyric has a strong affinity with the poems of Edgar Allan Poe. Nothing is known of either the composer or the lyricist.*

Macushla! Macushla! your sweet voice is calling,
Calling me softly again and again.
Macushla! Macushla! I hear its dear pleading,
My blue-eyed Macushla, I hear it in vain.

Macushla! Macushla! your white arms are reaching
I feel them enfolding, caressing me still.
Fling them out from the darkness, my lost love
        Macushla,
Let them find me and bind me again if they will.

Macushla! Macushla! your red lips are saying
That death is a dream and love is for aye.
Then awaken, Macushla, awake from your dreaming.
My blue-eyed Macushla, awaken to stay.

My Irish Molly, O

Billy Jerome

Great 1905 Tin-Pan-Alley hit for the homegrown Flanagan brothers, Joe and Michael, and since revived by Maura O'Connell.

Molly dear, and did you hear the news that's goin'
      round?
Down in the corner of my heart a loving place you
      found
And every time I gaze into your Irish eyes of blue,
They seem to whisper, 'Darlin' boy, my love is all for
      you.'

Chorus (to be repeated after each verse)
Molly – my Irish Molly – My sweet acushla dear,
I'm fairly off my trolley – my Irish Molly, when you are
      near,
Springtime you know is ring time,
Come dear, now don't be slow,
Change your name; g'wan be game,
Begorra and I'll do the same,
My Irish Molly, O.

Molly dear, and did you hear I've furnished up a flat:
Two little rooms, a fireplace, with a welcome on the
      mat,
Five pound down and two a week; we'll soon be out of
      debt.
It's all complete, except I haven't bought the cradle yet.

Molly dear, and did you hear what all the neighbours
        say
About the hundred sovereigns that you've safely stowed
        away:
They say that's why I love you; ah, but Molly that's a
        shame.
If you had only ninety-nine, I'd love you just the same!

Peggy O'Neill

Harry Pease, Edward G. Nelson and Gilbert Dodge

Another in a long line of danceable Irish colleens, with the patter chorus lending itself to a soft-shoe shuffle.

Peggy O'Neill is a girl who could steal
Any heart, anywhere any time
And I'll put you wise how you'll recognise
This wonderful girl of mine.

Chorus (to be repeated after each verse)
If her eyes are blue as skies
That's Peggy O'Neill.
If she's smiling all the while
That's Peggy O'Neill.
If she walks like a sly little rogue,
If she talks with a cute little brogue,
Sweet personality, full of rascality,
That's Peggy O'Neill.

Ev'rything's plann'd for a wedding so grand;
In the spring I will bring her the ring.
Then somewhere in town we'll both settle down
And all through the day I'll sing.

Alternative Patter Chorus (in triple time)

Annie Rooney sent a fellow looney but a million fellows
         now are feeling spooney
When they meet – Peggy O'Neill.
Molly-O was never, never slow but I want you to know
         she couldn't make a show
Along o' – sweet Peggy O'Neill.
Rose O'Grady was a perfect lady with a simple baby smile;
Peggy isn't simple that's why she has the other girlies beat a
         mile.
So if you meet a girl who's sweeter than Bedelia
And you feel you want to say, 'I'd like to steal yer!'
– That's Peggy O'Neill.

7

On Stage, Everybody

'They'se another scandal in th' Donahue family,' said Mr.
Dooley.
'What about?' asked Mr. McKenna eagerly.
'Molly give a vowdyvill,' replied Mr. Dooley.
'A what?'
'A-a vowdyvill.'
'What?'
'I tol' ye twice she gave a v'riety show,' said Mr Dooley angrily.
'Now d'ye know? She's been the leader iv society so long in the
sixth wa-ard that she was not to be downed be th' Hogans. They
gave a progressive spoil-five par-rty an' she med up her mind
she'd toss them over th' gashouse – socially, I mane – be havin'
a variety show.'
(*Mr Dooley:* Chicago Evening Post, *22 February 1896)*

Barney Brallaghan's Courtship

Peter K. Moran

One of a number of comic songs suitable for stage and parlour written by the Irish-born Moran who performed them with his Irish wife. The list of his 'dowry' though meant for comic effect was not far from the reality.

'Twas on a windy night, at two o'clock in the morning
An Irish lad so tight, all wind and weather scorning,
At Judy Callaghan's gate, sitting upon the paling
His love tale did relate and this was part of his
    wailing:

Chorus (to be repeated after each verse)
'Only say
You'll have Mister Brallaghan;
Don't say nay,
Charming Judy Callaghan.

'Ah, list to what I say: charms you've got like Venus.
Own your love you may; there's only a wall between
    us.
You lie fast asleep, snug in bed and snoring.
Round the house I creep, your hard heart imploring.

'I've got an old tomcat; thro' one eye he's staring,
I've got a Sunday hat, little the worse for wear.
I've got some gooseberry wine, the trees had got no
    riper on.
I've got a fiddle fine which only wants a piper on.

'I've got an acre of ground; I've got it set with
        potatoes.
I've got of baccy a pound; I've got some tea for the
        ladies;
I've got the ring to wed, some whiskey to make us
        gaily,
A mattress, feather bed and a handsome new shillelagh.

'You've got a charming eye; you've got some spelling
        and reading.
You've got, and so have I, a taste for genteel breeding;
You're rich and fair and young, as everybody's knowing
You've got a decent tongue whenever it's set a-going.

'For a wife till death I'm willing to take ye;
But, och, I waste my breath; I'm hoarse in trying to
        wake ye.
'Tis just beginning to rain; so I'll get under cover.
I'll come tomorrow again and be your constant lover.'

Dear Old Donegal

Attrib: Johnny Patterson

*Perennially popular 'returned Yank' song recorded with some
slight variation of text by Bing Crosby.*

It seems like only yesterday
    I left the cove of Cork,
An emigrant from Erin's Isle
    I landed in New York,
The divil a soul to meet me there
    A stranger on your shore
But Irish luck was with me
    And riches came galore.
And now I'm going back again
    To dear old Erin's Isle;
Me friends will meet me on the quay
    And greet me with a smile
Their faces, sure, I've almost forgot,
    I've been so long away
But me mother will introduce me
    And this to me will say:

Chorus (to be repeated after each verse)
Shake hands with your Uncle Mick, me boy,
    Shake hands with your sister Kate;
That's the girl you used to swing
    Down on the garden gate.
Shake hands with all the neighbours
    And kiss the colleens all
You're as welcome as the flowers in May
    To dear old Donegal.

They'll give a party when I go home
    And they'll come from near and far;
They'll line the roads for miles and miles
    With Irish jaunting cars
The tea and cake will be in galore
    To fill our hearts with joy
And the pipers will play an Irish reel
    To greet the Yankee boy.

We'll dance and sing the whole night long;
    Such fun was never seen.
The boys will be dressed in corduroys,
    The girls in ribbons green.
Their faces, sure, I've almost forgot,
    I've been so long away
But me mother will introduce me
    And this to me will say:

The Donevans

Edward Harrigan

'As sung by Harrigan and Hart with great success at Wallack's theatre, N. Y.'

We came from dear old Ireland,
We're strangers to this land;
We know that all Americans
Put forth their welcome hand
To the poor of suffering Ireland
Time and time again;
We thank you for your countrymen
And Donevan is our name.

Chorus (to be repeated after each verse)
We're the Donevans,
We're the Donevans
From the Emerald Isle
Across the sea.
We're the Donevans
From a noble family.

Our ancestors were noble
In the days of King O'Neal;
They fought for Erin's freedom
In a suit of silver mail!
Its Royal blood flows in our veins;
We're proud of that self-same—
We introduce ourselves to you:
Donevan is our name.

The Mulligan Guard

Edward Harrigan

First performed by Harrigan and his partner Tony Hart [Anthony J. Cannon (1855–1891)] in Chicago on 15 July 1873. It was the herald of many comic plays involving the Guards. The song was a skit on the target companies of the day, ostensibly paramilitary but essentially drinking companies.

We crave your condescension;
We'll tell you what we know
Of marching in the Mulligan Guard
From Sligo ward below.
Our captain's name was Hussey,
A Tipperary man;
He carried his sword like a Russian duke
Whenever he took command.

Chorus (to be repeated after each verse)
We shouldered guns, and march'd and march'd away
From Baxter Street to Avenue A
With drums and fife, how sweetly they did play
As we march'd, march'd, march'd in the Mulligan Guard.

When the band play'd Garry Owen,
Or the Connamara Pet;
With a rub-a-dub-dub, we'd march
In the mud, to a military step.
With the green above the red, boys,
To show where we come from,
Our guns we'd lift with the right shoulder shift
As we'd march to the bate of the drum.

Whin we got home at night, boys,
The divil a bit we'd ate;
We'd all set up and drink a sup
Of whiskey strong and nate.
Then we'd all march together,
As slippery as lard,
The solid min would all fall in
And march with the Mulligan Guard.

'Who Threw the Overalls in Mistress Murphy's Chowder?'

Words and Music by George L. Geifer

Comic vaudeville song written in 1898 by a one-hit wonder and given a boost by Phil Silvers in the film Coney Island *(1943). It was also recorded by Bing Crosby. The fact that the promised Hibernian ruction did not take place is an indication that the American Irish could at last laugh at themselves and had accepted American cuisine.*

Mistress Murphy gave a party just about a week ago
Everything was plentiful; the Murphys they're not slow.
They treated us like gentlemen; we tried to act the
        same;
Only for what happened – well it was an awful shame!
When Mrs Murphy dished the chowder she fainted on
        the spot.
She found a pair of overalls at the bottom of the pot.
Tim Nolan he got ripping mad; his eyes were bulging
        out.
He jumped up on the piano and loudly he did shout:

Chorus (to be repeated after each verse)
'Who threw the overalls in Mrs Murphy's chowder?'
No body spoke – so he shouted all the louder:
'It's an Irish trick that's true;
I can lick the Mick that threw
The overalls in Mistress Murphy's chowder.'

They dragged the pants from out the soup and laid
        them on the floor.

They were plastered up with mortar and were worn out
        at the knee.

They had their many ups and downs as we could
        plainly see

And when Mrs Murphy came to, she 'gan to cry and
        pout;

She had them in the wash that day and forgot to take
        them out.

Tim Nolan he excused himself for what he said that
        night.

So we put music to the words and sang with all our
        might:

Down Went McGinty

Joseph Flynn

Unrespectable but popular song of 1889 in spite of its enshrining all the undesirable attributes of the stage American/Irishman. It spawned a flood of even worse 'Mc Ginty' songs. It suggested the appropriate title for the Preston Sturges film The Great McGinty *(1940) about an Irish tramp who becomes governor of a state.*

Sunday morning just at nine,
Dan McGinty dressed so fine,
Stood looking up at a very high stone wall;
When his friend young Pat McCann
Says, 'I'll bet five dollars, Dan,
I could carry you to the top without a fall.'
So on his shoulders he took Dan;
To climb the ladder he began
And he soon commenced to reach up near the top
When McGinty, cute old rogue,
To win the five he did let go
Never thinking just how far he'd have to drop . . .

First Chorus
Down went McGinty to the bottom of the wall
And though he won the five
He was more dead than alive;
Sure his ribs and nose and back were broke
From getting such a fall,
Dress'd in his best suit of clothes!

From the hospital Mac went home
When they fix'd his broken bones
To find he was the father of a child;
So to celebrate it right
His friends he went to invite
And he soon was drinking whiskey fast and wild.
Then he waddled down the street,
In his Sunday suit so neat,
Holding up his head as proud as John the Great
But in the sidewalk was a hole,
To receive a ton of coal,
That McGinty never saw till just too late . . .

Second Chorus
Down went McGinty to the bottom of the hole.
Then the driver of a cart
Gave the load of coal a start
And it took us half an hour
To dig McGinty from the coal,
Dress'd in his best suit of clothes!

Now McGinty raved and swore;
About his clothes he felt so sore
And an oath he took he'd kill the man or die.
So he tightly grabb'd his stick
And hit the driver a lick;
Then he raised a little shanty on his eye;
But two policemen saw the muss
And they soon joined in the fuss.
Then they ran McGinty in for being drunk;
The judge says with a smile,
'We'll keep you for a while
In a cell to sleep upon a prison bunk . . .

Third Chorus
Down went McGinty to the bottom of the jail
Where his board would cost him nix
And he stay'd exactly six;
They were big long months he stopped
For no one went his bail . . .
Dress'd in his best suit of clothes!

Now McGinty, thin and pale,
One fine day got out of jail
And with joy to see his boy was nearly wild;
To his house he quickly ran
To meet his wife Bedaley Ann
But she'd skipped away and took along the child.
Then he gave up in despair
And he madly pulled his hair,
As he stood one day upon the river shore,
Knowing well he couldn't swim
He did foolishly jump in
Although water he had never took before . . .

Fourth Chorus
Down went McGinty to the bottom of the say
And he must be very wet
For they haven't found him yet;
But they say his ghost comes round the docks
Before the break of day . . .
Dress'd in his best suit of clothes!

Harrigan

George M. Cohan

Cohan's 1907 tribute to an older songwriting colleague Ned Harrigan who, with his partner Tony Hart, were the leading 'Irish' performers in late-nineteenth-century vaudeville theatres.

Who is the man who will spend or will even lend?
    Harrigan, That's me!
Who is your friend when you finds you need a friend?
    Harrigan, That's me!
For I'm just as proud of my name you see
    As an emperor or tsar or a king could be:
Who is the man helps a man ev'ry time he can?
    Harrigan, That's me!

Chorus (to be repeated after each verse)
H – A – double R– I – G – A - N spells Harrigan
Proud of all the Irish blood that's in me;
Divil a man can say a word agin me.
H – A – double R– I – G – A - N spells Harrigan, you
    see;
It's a name that shame never been connected with.
Harrigan, that's me!

Who is the man never stood for a gadabout?
Harrigan, That's me!
Who is the man that the town's simply mad about?
Harrigan, That's me!
The ladies and babies are fond of me;
I'm fond of them, too, in return, you see.
Who is the gent that's deserving a monument?
Harrigan, That's me!

If We Only Had Old Ireland Over Here

Anon

*Americanised version of a song originally set in Australia,
resulting in total geographical and psychological confusion.*

I was dreaming of old Ireland and Killarney's lakes and
    dells;
I was dreaming of the shamrock and the dear old
    Shandon bells,
When memory suggested in a vision bright and fair
Of the strange things that would happen if we had old
    Ireland here.

Chorus (to be repeated after each verse)
If the Blarney stone stood out on Station Island
And Dublin town to Brooklyn came to stay,
If the Shannon water joined the Hudson river,
And Killarney's lakes flowed into Rockaway,
If the Shandon bells rang out in old Manhattan
And County Cork at New York did appear,
Erin's sons would never roam, all the boys would stay at
    home,
If we only had old Ireland over here.

There are lots of lovely fairies dancing on the village
    green
And there are lots of lovely colleens, the finest ever
    seen,
Where the boys are all called Paddy and the girls are
    Molly dear;
Sure we'd wrap the green flag round them, if we had
    old Ireland here.

8

A Great Day for the Irish

Ar-re ye ready? Play up th' wearin' iv the green, ye baloon-headed Dutchmin. Hannigan, go an' get the polis to intherfere – th' Sons of St Patrick an' th' Ancient Order's come together. Glory be, me saddle's slippin'. Ar-re ye ready? For-wa-rd, march!'

(Mr. Dooley: Chicago Evening Post, *21 March 1896)*

Maggie Murphy's Home

Edward Harrigan

Harrigan's famous tribute to the slowly upwardly mobile Irish of the New York slums. It was written in 1890 for a play Reilly and the Four Hundred.

Behind a grammar schoolhouse,
In a double tenement,
I live with my old mother
And always pay the rent.
A bedroom and a parlour
Is what we call our own
And you're welcome ev'ry evening
At Maggie Murphy's home.

Chorus (to be repeated after each verse)
On Sunday night, 'tis my delight
And pleasure don't you see:
Meeting all the girls and all the boys
That work downtown with me.
There's an organ in the parlour
To give the house a tone;
And you're welcome every evening
At Maggie Murphy's home.

Such dancing in the parlor;
There's a waltz for you and I;
Such mashing in the stairway
And kisses on the sly.
God bless the leisure hours
That working people know
And they're welcome ev'ry evening
At Maggie Murphy's home.

It's from the open window
At the noontime of the day,
You'll see the neighbours' children
So happy in their play.
There's Jimmy with his Nelly
Together romp and roam
And they gather near the schoolyard
Near Maggie Murphy's home.

As I walk thro' Hogan's Alley
At the closing of the day
To greet my dear old mother,
You'll hear the neighbours say,
'Oh! there goes little Maggie.
I wish she were my own;
Oh! may blessings ever linger
On Maggie Murphy's home.'

Muldoon, The Solid Man

Edward Harrigan

Harrigan's most famous song, a portrait of the successful Irish emigrant who rose to affluence by brains and political opportunism, first sung by its author in 1874.

I am a man of great influence
And educated to a high degree.
I came here whin small from Donegal;
In the *Daniel Webster* across the sea.
In the sixth ward I situated
In a tenement house with my brother Dan
By perseverance I elevated
And wint to the front like a solid man.

Chorus (to be repeated after each verse)
So come with me and I'll use you dacent.
I'll get you drunk and I'll fill your can.
As I walk the street each friend I meet
Says, 'There goes Muldoon; he's a solid man.'

To every party and every raffle
I always go, an invited guest;
As conspicuous as General Grant, boys
I wear a rosebud upon my breast;
I'm called upon to address the meeting,
Without regard to clique or clan.
I show the Constitution wid elocution
Because, you know, I'm a solid man.

I control the Tombs, I control the Island.
My constituents, they all go there
To enjoy the summer's recreation
And the refreshing East River air.
I'm known in Harlem; I'm known in Jersey;
I'm welcome hearty on every hand;
Wid my regalay on Patrick's Day
I march away like a solid man.

Extra Chorus
For oppositions or politicians,
Take my word, I don't give a damn.
As I walk the street each friend I meet
Says, 'There goes Muldoon; he's a solid man.'

The Band Played On

John F. Palmer

Song written in 1895 by Palmer, a New York actor, and made popular in vaudeville performance by its composer and publisher. Its extreme popularity with a million copies of the sheet music sold has given the title an almost proverbial resonance.

Matt Casey formed a social club that beat the town for
     style
  And hired for a meeting-place a hall.
When pay-day came around each week they greased
     the floor with wax
  And danced with noise and vigour at the ball.
Each Saturday you'd see them dressed up in Sunday
     clothes;
  Each lad would have his sweetheart by his side.
When Casey led the first grand march they all would
     fall in line,
  Behind the man who was her joy and pride – For

Chorus (to be repeated after each verse)
Casey would waltz with a strawberry blonde and the band
     played on.
He'd glide cross the floor with the girl he ador'd and the
     band played on
But his brain was so loaded it nearly exploded
The poor girl would shake with alarm.
He'd ne'er leave the girl with the strawberry curls
And the band played on.

Such kissing in the corner and such whisp'ring in the
  hall
  And telling tales of love behind the stairs.
As Casey was the favourite and he that ran the hall,
  Of kissing and love-making did his share.
At twelve o'clock exactly they all would fall in line
  Then march down to the dining-hall and eat.
But Casey would not join them although everything
  was fine
  But he stayed upstairs and exercised his feet – For

Now when the dance was over and the band played
  'Home, Sweet Home'
  They played a tune at Casey's own request.
He thank'd them very kindly for the favours they had
  shown,
  Then he'd waltz once with the girl that he loved
  best.
Most all the friends were married that Casey used to
  know
  And Casey too has taken him a wife.
The blonde he used to waltz and glide with on the
  ballroom floor
  Is happy Mrs. Casey now for life – For

Final Chorus
Casey would waltz with a strawberry blonde and the band
  played on.
He'd glide cross the floor with the girl he ador'd and the
  band played on
But his brain was so loaded it nearly exploded
The poor girl would shake with alarm.
He married the girl with the strawberry curls
And the band played on.

Casey at the Bat

Ernest Lawrence Thayer

Famous anti-climactic American comic poem that haunted its reluctant author.

The outlook wasn't brilliant for the Mudville nine that
      day:
The score stood four to two with but one inning more
      to play.
And then when Cooney died at first, and Barrows did
      the same,
A sickly silence fell upon the patrons of the game.

A straggling few got up to go in deep despair. The rest
Clung to that hope which springs eternal in the human
      breast;
They thought if only Casey could but get a whack at
      that –
We'd put up even money now with Casey at the bat.

But Flynn preceded Casey, as did also Jimmy Blake,
And the former was a lulu and the latter was a cake;
So upon that stricken multitude grim melancholy sat,
For there seemed but little chance of Casey's getting to
      the bat.

But Flynn let drive a single, to the wonderment of all,
And Blake, the much despisèd, tore the cover off the
      ball;
And when the dust had lifted, and the men saw what
      had occurred,
There was Jimmy safe at second and Flynn a-hugging
      third.

Then from 5000 throats and more there rose a lusty
   yell;
It rumbled through the valley, it rattled in the dell;
It knocked upon the mountain and recoiled upon the
   flat,
For Casey, mighty Casey, was advancing to the bat.

There was ease in Casey's manner as he stepped into
   his place;
There was pride in Casey's bearing and a smile on
   Casey's face.
And when, responding to the cheers, he lightly doffed
   his hat,
No stranger in the crowd could doubt 'twas Casey at
   the bat.

And now the leather-covered sphere came hurtling
   through the air,
And Casey stood a-watching it with haughty grandeur
   there.
Close by the sturdy batsman the ball unheeded sped –
'That ain't my style,' said Casey. 'Strike one,' the
   umpire said.

From the benches black with people, there went up a
   muffled roar,
Like the beating of the storm-waves on a stern and
   distant shore.
'Kill him! Kill the umpire!' shouted someone in the
   stand;
And likely they'd have killed him had not Casey raised
   his hand.

With a smile of Christian charity great Casey's visage
     shone;
He stilled the rising tumult; he bade the game go on;
He signaled to the pitcher, and once more the spheroid
     flew;
But Casey still ignored it, and the umpire said 'Strike
     two.'

'Fraud!' cried the maddened thousands, and the echo
     answered fraud;
But one scornful look from Casey and the audience was
     awed.
They saw his face grow stern and cold, they saw his
     muscles strain,
And they knew that Casey wouldn't let that ball go by
     again.

The sneer is gone from Casey's lip, his teeth are
     clenched in hate;
He pounds with cruel violence his bat upon the plate.
And now the pitcher holds the ball, and now he lets it
     go,
And now the air is shattered by the force of Casey's
     blow.

Oh, somewhere in this favored land the sun is shining
     bright;
The band is playing somewhere, and somewhere hearts
     are light,
And somewhere men are laughing, and somewhere
     children shout;
But there is no joy in Mudville – mighty Casey has
     struck out.

When Irish Eyes Are Smiling

Chauncey Olcott and George Graff

Perennial favourite with bar-room singers since its first airing in The Isle o' Dreams *(1913).*

There's a tear in your eye and I'm wonderin' why,
For it never should be there at all.
With such pow'r in your smile, sure a stone you'd
      beguile;
So there's never a teardrop should fall.
When your sweet lilting laughter's like some fairy song
And your eyes twinkle bright as can be
You should laugh all the while and all other times
And now smile a smile for me.

Chorus (to be repeated after each verse)
When Irish eyes are smiling sure it's like a morn in spring.
In the lilt of Irish laughter you can hear the angels sing.
When Irish hearts are happy all the world seems bright and
    gay
And when Irish eyes are smiling sure they'd steal your heart
    away.

For your smile is a part of the love in your heart
And it makes even sunshine more bright.
Like the linnet's sweet song, crooning all the day long,
Comes your laughter so tender and light.
For the springtime of life is the sweetest of all;
There is ne'er a real care or regret
And while springtime is yours throughout all of youth's
      hours,
Let us smile each chance we get.

It's a Great Day for the Irish

Roger Edens

Song specially written to be sung by Judy Garland in the film
Little Nellie Kelly *(1940).*

Oh I woke me up this morning and I heard a joyful
      song
From the throats of happy Irishmen, a hundred
      thousand strong;
Shure it was the Hibernian Brigade,
Lining up for to start the big parade.
So I fetched me Sunday bonnet, and the flag I love so
      well
And I bought meself a shamrock just to wear in me
      lapel.
Don't you know that today's March seventeen?
It's the day for the wearing of the green!

Chorus
It's a great day for the Irish; it's a great day for a fair!
The sidewalks of New York are thick with blarney;
For shure you'd think New Yark was all Killarney!
It's a great day for the shamrock, for the flags in full array.
We're feeling so inspirish, shure because for all the Irish
It's a great, great day!

Repeat Chorus
It's a great day for the Irish; it's a great day for fair!
Be gosh, there's not a cop to stop a raiding;
Begorra all the cops are out parading.
It's a great day for the shamrock, for the flags in full array.
And as we go a swinging, ev'ry Irish heart is singing:
'It's a great, great day!'

Biographical Index

The following list is necessarily incomplete since in many instances little more than the name of an author is known.

Dion(ysius Lardner) Boucicault was born in Dublin in 1820. He dropped out of London University to become an actor and in time the most prolific playwright of the nineteenth century. Of his 150 plays three set in Ireland, *The Colleen Bawn* (1860), *Arrah na Pogue* (1864) and *The Shaughraun* (1874) are still popular. In keeping with contemporary practice he filled his plays with songs, thus preserving some that might have otherwise been lost. He died in New York in 1890.

Teresa Brayton was born Boylan at Kilbrook, near Cloncurry, County Kildare in 1868 and qualified as a teacher. She emigrated to America when she was twenty and wrote poems as T.B. Kilbrook. She married Richard Brayton and was a regular visitor to Ireland. She was a friend of Patrick Pearse and died in Bray, County Wicklow in the 1920s.

J. Keirn Brennan was born in 1873 and died in 1948. An American of Irish extraction, he is remembered as the lyricist of several popular songs including 'A Little Bit of Heaven', 'Empty Saddles' and the deservedly lesser-known 'She's the Daughter of Mother Machree' and 'Goodbye, Mother Machree'.

Thomas Casey was a Tammany entertainer of the 1880s and 1890s who is remembered as the author of the chauvinistic song of the American-Irish workman 'Drill, Ye Tarriers'.

'Claribel' [Charlotte Alington] was born in Louth, Lincolnshire in 1830 and unusually for the period was encouraged by her husband Charles Barnard to continue her career as composer and lyricist of many songs including 'Come Back To Erin', which is still a popular parlour piece. She died in Dover in 1869.

Joseph Ignatius Constantine Clarke was born in Kingstown in 1846 and joined the Board of Trade in 1863, resigning five years later 'for patriotic reasons.' Afterwards he had a distinguished career as a journalist and editor in America. He wrote one the many nineteenth-century plays about Robert Emmet in 1888 and a verse drama called *Malmorda* in 1893 which begins; 'To me by early morn/Came memories of old Ireland by the sea.' He died in 1925.

Maggie Cline was a literally loud-mouthed Irish-American entertainer who turned the scales at 230 lbs. Her deep contralto could effortlessly overcome the noise in the burlesque halls where in the 1890s she sang such 'male' songs as 'Drill, Ye Tarriers, 'Down Went McGinty' and 'Throw Him Down, McCloskey'.

George M(ichael) Cohan was born in Providence, Rhode Island in 1878 and first appeared on the stage at the age of ten with his parents and sister as the Four Cohans. He wrote many popular and patriotic Broadway shows including *Little Johnny Jones* (1904) and *Little Nellie Kelly* (1922). His songs, including 'Forty-five Minutes from Broadway', 'Mary's a Grand Old Name', 'Give My Regards to Broadway', 'Yankee Doodle Boy' and the war song 'Over There', were featured in the biopic *Yankee Doodle Dandy* (1942) in which he was brilliantly impersonated by James Cagney (1899–1986). He died in 1942.

Julia Crawford was born Louise Matilda Jane Montague perhaps in County Cavan in 1799. She wrote many songs and novels, all of which have now lapsed into obscurity except the unsinkable 'Kathleen Mavourneen'. She died in 1860.

Al Dubin was born in Zurich in 1891 and died in New York in 1945. He was taken to America in 1893 and became a noted lyricist for songs for the new Talkies, notably the famous *42nd Street* (1933).

Helen Selina, Lady Dufferin was born in London in 1807, the granddaughter of Sheridan the dramatist (1751–1816). She married the 4th Marquis of Dufferin and Ava, and in the family's lands near Newtownards, County Down there is still a memorial tower to her memory. She died in 1867.

Finley Peter Dunne was born in Chicago in 1867, the son of Irish immigrants, and began a career in journalism when he was sixteen, having graduated last in his high school class. In 1893, he began writing a column for the *Chicago Evening Post* in the character of Mr Dooley, a saloonkeeper in the Irish working-class district of Bridgeport and for the next seven years grew to national fame because of the wit and wisdom and subtle language, spoken in an apparently impenetrable Irish brogue of his creation. After 1898 Dunne left Chicago for New York and Mr Dooley moved too, becoming a national but less effective commentator on life, liberty and the pursuit of Americanism continuing his musings for a further fifteen years. Dunne died in New York in 1936, 'the first voice of genius in Irish-American literature'.

Maurice Francis Egan was born in Philadelphia in 1852, the son of an Irish father, a pre-Famine immigrant from Tipperary. He graduated from La Salle College in that city and went on to become a leading Catholic journalist, author and academic, serving as professor of English Literature in Notre Dame and the Catholic University of Washington. He wrote many novels about 'respectable' Irish-Americans and was American Minister to Denmark, 1907–1918. He died in 1924.

Edmund Falconer was born Edmund O'Rourke in Dublin in 1814 and went on stage as a boy. He was the original Danny Mann in Boucicault's *The Colleen Bawn* (1960) and the author of many plays himself. His parlour piece 'Killarney' is still sung. He died in London in 1879.

Joseph Flynn was one half of a rowdy Irish variety act in the 1880s and 1890s. He is remembered now only as the writer of the rumbustious song 'Down Went McGinty'.

[William] Percy French was born in Cloonyquin, County Roscommon in 1854 and after a leisurely career as an undergraduate student of engineering at Trinity was appointed 'Inshpector of Drains' for County Cavan. He began writing songs while still at school and supplemented his income with comic sketches in the entirely self-written paper *The Jarvey*. On the death of his first wife he became Ireland's most famous travelling entertainer, using his skills as an instrumentalist and water-colourist as well as the performance of his own brilliant songs and recitations which judiciously combined humour and sentimentality to entrance a generation of Irish audiences. He was the author of the 'traditional American college song "Abdulla Bulbul Ameer"'. He died in Formby, Lancashire, in 1920.

Alice Furlong was born in County Dublin about 1875 and gained a national reputation as a poet whose subject was the Ireland of her maturity. She died in 1946.

Charles Graham Halpine was born in County Meath in 1829, the son of a clergyman. He emigrated to America in 1851 and became a journalist in New York. He joined the Federal army on the outbreak of the Civil War and rose to the rank of brigadier-general in the famous 'Fighting 69th'. Earlier he recruited and commanded the first Afro-American regiment. He wrote two novels and many songs and poems, such as 'Private Myles O'Reilly', and died from an accidental overdose of chloral taken to cure a cold in 1868.

Edward Harrigan, the great star of Irish-American vaudeville and comic theatre, was born in New York in 1845 and ran away from home to go on the stage. He teamed up with Tony Hart [Anthony J. Cannon] (1855–91) who played the wife Cordelia to his Dan Mulligan in a very popular series of shows from 1872–84. He wrote thirty-nine plays and many songs including 'The Mulligan Guards', 'Muldoon, the Solid Man', and 'Maggie Murphy's Home' with music by his father-in-law Dave Braham. He died in 1911, having last appeared on stage in 1908.

William Jerome was born in 1865 and died in 1932. He was for many years a successful song lyricist with songs numbers to his credit, such as 'Chinatown, My Chinatown', 'Heart of My Heart', 'My Irish Molly' and 'Sweet Rosie O'Grady'.

John W. Kelly ('The Rolling Mill Man') was a mill-worker turned songwriter who performed such popular favourites as 'Throw Him Down, McCloskey' in the last quarter of the nineteenth century.

William Kenneally was born in Cloyne, County Cork, in 1828 and had a career in journalism in Tipperary and Kilkenny (where her served for a term as mayor). He wrote verse under the pseudonym 'William of Munster' and is remembered now for 'The Moon behind the Hill' which gained great popularity with Irish-Americans in minstrel shows. He died in 1876.

Louis Lambert (Patrick Sarsfield Gilmore) was born in Athlone in 1829 but became a bandmaster and impresario in America in the 1850s. He and the entire Gilmore band enlisted in 1861 but by 1862 were reverted to the safer duties of troop entertainment. His famous song 'When Johnny Comes Marching Home' was written in anticipation of the end of the war which he survived to organise the Peace Jubilee in Boston in 1869. This featured a orchestra of 1,000, a chorus of 10,000 and many distinguished visitors including the younger Strauss. He died in St Louis, Missouri in 1892.

John Locke was born in Callan, County Kilkenny in 1847. He joined the IRB in 1863 and contributed to James Stephens' Fenian journal the *Irish People*. He had the characteristic IRB career of journalism, imprisonment and exile in America. He died in New York in 1889.

Samuel Lover was born in Dublin in 1797, the son of a stockbroker, and trained as a painter, was elected to the Royal Hibernian Academy in 1828. When his eyesight began to fail he turned to literature, writing *Legends and Stories of Ireland* (1831) and the comic novel *Handy Andy*

(1842). He devised a theatrical entertainment *An Irish Evening*, for which he wrote the songs and sketches. He received a Civil List pension in 1856 and died in St. Helier, Jersey, in 1868.

James Gaspard Maedar was born in Ireland in 1809 and began his musical career in London. He was a significant figure in New York musical circles in 1827 when he married the actress Clara Fisher (1811–98) whose career stretched from child prodigy to grande dame. She appeared in operetta as well as classical parts and sang her husband's songs, notably the nostalgic 'Teddy O'Neale'. He died in 1876.

William McBurney was born in County Down in 1844. He emigrated to America and worked as a journalist, dying in 1892. He contributed to the *Nation* as 'Carroll Malone'.

Thomas D'Arcy McGee was born in Carlingford, County Louth in 1828. He emigrated to America at seventeen and became editor of the *Boston Eagle* in 1846. Once an ardent Young Irelander, he ceased to support revolution after the abortive rising of Smith O'Brien in 1848 and became a bitter foe of the IRB and Fenianism. This may have been the cause of his assassination in Canada in 1868. He had had a ten-year career in politics there.

Peter K. Moran was probably born in Ireland about 1800 and by the 1830s had established himself in New York where he and his wife gave concerts. He wrote a number of comic Irish songs including 'Cruiskeen Lawn' and 'Barney Brallaghan's Courtship'.

William Mulchinock was born near Tralee, County Kerry in 1820. Although a Protestant he was a supporter of Daniel O'Connell and had to flee the country after an affray for which he was held responsible. He returned to Ireland in 1846 and died in 1864. He is remembered as the author of 'The Rose of Tralee' which he wrote for a lost sweetheart.

Joseph O'Connor was born in Tribes Hill, New York in 1841 and became a journalist. His brother Michael (1837–62), also a poet, was killed in the Civil War and some of Joseph's poems reflect that trauma.

Chauncey Olcott [John Chancellor] was born in Buffalo, New York in 1858 and began his stage career as a member of a black-face minstrel troupe in 1876. He appeared several times in London while studying singing and on his return to the USA began to star in a number of Irish musical plays which he also wrote. A composer as well as lyricist, he had a hand in 'Mother Machree' and other popular Irish songs including 'When Irish Eyes Are Smiling' and 'My Wild Irish Rose' the latter of which he wrote, composed and sang and which gave the title to his 1947 biopic with Denis Morgan. He died in Monte Carlo in 1932.

John Boyle O'Reilly was born at Dowth Castle in County Meath in 1844 and became a Fenian organiser in the British army. Arrested in 1863, he was sentenced to death but was transported after much harsh treatment to Australia. He escaped, made his way to America and became a radical editor and joint-owner of the *Boston Pilot* making it a kind of transatlantic *Nation*. He died in 1890, like Charles Halpine, of an accidental drug overdose.

Johnny Patterson was born in Feakle, County Clare in 1840 and became a famous circus clown, appearing in America with the Ringling Brothers. He is also credited with the authorship of many popular Irish songs including 'The Stone Outside Dan Murphy's Door' and 'The Garden where the Praties Grow'. He was killed in Tralee in 1889 in an affray at a Parnellite meeting.

John James Piatt was born in Indiana in 1835 and after a civil service career during the Civil War, became librarian of the House of Representatives and American consul in Cork (1882–94). Like Browning, he married another poet, Sarah Morgan, and separately they published much verse. He died in 1917.

Ernest Lawrence Thayer was born in Lawrence, Massachusetts in 1863 and majored in philosphy at Harvard. It was there that he developed the obsession with baseball that led to his one 'hit', 'Casey at the Bat', which haunted him for the rest of his business life as manager of the family woollen mills in Worcester in his home state. He died in 1940.

Fred(eric) E(dward) Weatherly was born in Somerset in 1848 and educated at Brasenose College, Oxford, where he later worked as a crammer for twenty years. He was called to the Bar in 1887 and became an expert on copyright. He composed the first English versions of *Cav* and *Pag*, which contains the famous line: 'On with the motley, the paint and the powder'. He is the lyricist of 1,500 songs including 'Roses of Picardy' and 'Danny Boy'. He died in 1929.

Thomas P. Westendorf was born in Indiana in 1848 and qualified as a doctor. He is famous as the author of the hugely successful 'I'll Take You Home Again, Kathleen'. He also wrote 'Goodbye, Mavourneen'. He died in 1923.

Rida Johnson Young was born in Baltimore in 1865 and became a leading librettist for Broadway shows, writing lyrics for Jerome Kern (1885–1945), Rudolf Friml (1879–1972) and the Irish-born Victor Herbert (1859–1924). Her two most famous songs were 'Ah, Sweet Mystery of Life' and 'Mother Machree'. She died in Stamford, Connecticut in 1926.

Index of Titles

Index of First Lines

Molly dear, and did you hear the news that's goin' round, 131
My feet are here on Broadway this blessed harvest morn, 27
My name is Macnamara; I'm the leader of the band, 88
My name is Paddy Leary, 25
Now Clancy was a peaceful man if you know what I mean, 116
Now the ship it sails in half an hour, 33
O Paddy dear, and did you hear the news that's goin' round, 93
O'Ryan was a man of might, 97
Och man dear, did you ever hear of purty Molly Brallaghan, 120
Oh Danny Boy, the pipes, the pipes are calling, 46
Oh I woke me up this morning and I heard a joyful song, 163
Oh! ev'ry morn at seven o'clock, 65
Oh! Molly Bawn, why leave me pining, 119
Oh, 'twas there I larned readin' and writin', 111
Peggy O'Neill is a girl who could steal, 133
'Read out the names,' and Burke sat back, 104
Sunday morning just at nine, 146
Sure we're the boys from County Clare, 78
Th'anam an Dhia but there it is, 43
The general dashed along the road, 107
The outlook wasn't brilliant for the Mudville nine that day, 159
The pale moon was rising above the green mountain, 124
There's a spot in me heart that no colleen may own, 56
There's a tear in your eye and I'm wonderin' why, 162
'Twas down at Dan McDevitt's at the corner of this street, 113
'Twas down by Boston Harbour I carelessly did stray, 108
'Twas on a windy night, at two o'clock in the morning, 137
Tim Finnegan lived in Walkin Street, 86
We came from dear old Ireland, 141
We crave your condescension, 142
When April rains make flowers bloom, 49
When I landed in sweet Philadelphia, 69
When Johnny comes marching home again, hurrah, hurrah, 99
Who is the man who will spend or will even lend, 148
Will you come to the bower o'er the free boundless ocean, 109

Bibliography

D'Arcy, F. *The Story of Irish Emigration*. Dublin/Cork, 1999.

Dunne, F. P. *Mr Dooley and the Chicago Irish*. (ed. C. Fanning). Washington DC, 1987.

Fanning, C. *The Irish Voice in America*. Lexington, Kentucky, 1990.

Gammond, P. *The Oxford Companion to Popular Music*. Oxford, 1991.

Stedman, E. C. (ed.) *An American Anthology*. Boston, 1901.

Williams, W. H. A. *'Twas Only an Irishman's Dream*. Chicago, 1996.

Wright, R. L. (ed.) *Irish Emigrant Ballads and Songs*. Bowling Green, Ohio, 1975.

Acknowledgements

The publishers are grateful for permission to reproduce copyright material:

'A Little Bit of Heaven, Shure They Call it Ireland': Words and music by J. Keirn Brennan and Ernest R. Ball © 1914, M. Witmark & Sons, USA, and B. Feldman & Co Ltd; ''Twas Only an Irishman's Dream': Words and music by John O'Brien, Al Dubin and Rennie Cormack © 1916, M. Witmark & Sons, USA, and B. Feldman & Co Ltd; 'My Wild Irish Rose': Words and music by Chauncey Olcott © 1899, M. Witmark & Sons, USA, and B. Feldman & Co Ltd; 'My Irish Molly O': Words and music by William Jerome and Jean Schwartz © 1905, Remick Music Corp, USA, and Francis Day & Hunter Ltd; 'Peggy O'Neill': Words and music by Harry Pease, Gilbert Dodge and Ed G. Nelson © 1921 EMI Catalogue Partnership and EMI Feist Catalog Inc, USA; 'Harrigan': Words and music by George M. Cohan © 1907, EB Marks Music Corp, USA, and B Feldman & Co Ltd; 'When Irish Eyes Are Smiling': Words and music by Chauncey Olcott, George Graff and Ernest R. Ball © 1912, M. Witmark & Sons, USA, and B. Feldman & Co Ltd; 'It's A Great Day for the Irish': Words and music by Roger Edens © 1940 EMI Catalogue Partnership and EMI Feist Catalog Inc, USA. All reproduced by permission of International Music Publications Ltd.